An O'Mara's Reunion

Book 13, The Guesthouse on the Green

Michelle Vernal

Copyright © 2022 by Michelle Vernal

All rights reserved.

No portion of this book, An O'Mara's Reunion may be reproduced in any form without written permission from the publisher or author, except as permitted by U.S. copyright law.

Chapter One

July, 2002

'Close would yer,' Roisin muttered, attempting to zip shut the wheelie case she'd just finished packing for her trip to Ireland. The bulging carry-on was on her bed, and she regretted not making Mammy splurge for checked-in luggage when she'd booked her and Noah's flight from Heathrow to Dublin.

Her current mood was not good, and it wasn't solely down to the case not doing her bidding. She was disgruntled over Mammy's sneakiness in roping her and Noah into this four-day jaunt. Their first and last night would be spent at O'Mara's in Dublin, which was grand. She was excited to see her nieces and nephew. The two in between, however, would be spent in a village called Claredoncally in County Cork. The reason for this was an O'Mara family reunion. Why it couldn't have been held in civilisation, Roisin didn't know. The idea of being stuck with all those culchies was scary enough, but the thought of O'Mara relatives gathering en masse was scarier. Most disappointingly, too, was that Uncle Cormac and his partner Ricardo – who'd have made the gathering bearable by adding a splash of colour – couldn't make it.

Mammy had rung Roisin a few weeks ago to enquire whether she fancied a weekend away to a charmingly rural hotspot with her sisters. It was worded as if she were offering an all-expenses spa trip to a posh resort in the country. A thank-you for blessing her with grandchildren and being the best daughters a Mammy could have. Roisin had instantly drifted off into a lovely daydream where Mammy had volunteered to mind Noah, Kiera and the twins for the weekend, leaving Roisin and her sisters to their own devices. Long lunches with wine flowing would be enjoyed between massages and facials — all paid for by Mammy, of course.

'Roisin, are you there?' Mammy demanded.

'I'd love a weekend away, so I would, Mammy,' had been her dreamy response.

Sadly, the daydream was shattered when Mammy announced she'd RSVP to Noreen on Roisin and Noah's behalf. It wasn't an all-expenses weekend away sans children on offer, and warily she'd asked, 'What do you mean. RSVP to Noreen?' The only Noreen she knew was Great Aunt Noreen, who wasn't, in fact, an aunt at all, but nobody knew what else to call her.

'To the reunion, of course.'

'Mammy, what reunion?' Roisin's voice had grown demanding as she'd felt the noose tighten.

'Rosi, Rosi, Rosi.'

'I know my name. Thanks very much, Mammy.'

'I'm talking about the O'Mara family reunion. I told you yer Great Aunt Noreen was organising a shindig when we were waiting for the twins' arrival at the hospital.'

Roisin dimly recalled Mammy prattling on about the O'Mara side of the family meeting up. At the time, she'd been sat in the waiting room alongside Moira, Tom and Shay, biting her lip as Mammy's words floated in one ear and out the other. This wasn't an unusual occurrence by any means. Now, though, she was regretting not paying attention. If she'd listened, she could have been on the ball with an excuse at the ready. Aisling and Moira would be hearing from her too. Her sisters should have given her the heads-up about what was being plotted.

The whole thing was ridiculous, anyway, because family reunions weren't held on drop-everything notice. Nor were they held in the Irish wilderness. Except, it would seem, when the hostess and her awful niece decided to rally the troops by inviting them to a village so small it didn't get a mention on the map.

'There's a big difference between talking and doing, Mam,' Roisin argued desperately. 'Besides, didn't we have a grand catch-up with Noreen and Emer in Los Angeles? Sure, that was only two years ago.'

'There have been babbies born since then,' Maureen had stated. 'And, I, for one, am looking forward to it. I'm particularly excited about seeing your father's second cousin removed, Bernice, again. She was always a snooty wan who thought herself above your father and me. Her family owned a house in County Cork almost as big as her nose. I've been amassing photographs of myself and Donal's sea view to show her.'

Roisin had rolled her eyes.

Now here she was with her tongue poking out the corner of her mouth as she tried to wrest the zipper around the tricky corner of her case. The only bonus of this trip across the sea was that Shay was coming to the reunion as her plus one. He was away at the moment in Germany overseeing an electronic music festival, but flew back in late Friday night. He'd take an early-morning flight to Cork and pick up a car at the airport to drive to Claredoncally.

Roisin had decided, once she'd thought about it properly, that there were two other bonuses. First, Mammy's three brothers, the Brothers Grimm as they were otherwise known, wouldn't be there because they weren't O'Maras. Secondly, Claredoncally's only hotel boasted a firm no-pets policy. As such, Noah's gerbils, Mr Nibbles and Steve (who'd surprised them all by being a Stef) would not be able to come with them. Every cloud had a silver lining and all that.

'Mummy, you've got too much in your case.' Noah interrupted her thoughts as he materialised in the doorway of her bedroom. Today he was dressed in shorts with the big pockets he liked on the sides, and – surprise, surprise – his favourite Mickey Mouse tee shirt, which was too small.

Roisin glanced down at her green tank top with its yellow daisy emblem and decided not to remark. Noah's tee shirt had been bought by his nana on the family's trip to Disneyland. It had swamped him initially, with Maureen announcing he'd plenty of room to grow into it. But, two years later, he'd well and truly outgrown it. It was his favourite, however, and when Roisin had told him it was time to donate the shirt to one of the local charity shops, he'd been horrified. The result was he'd taken to wearing the shirt any chance he got lest his mother swiped it when his back was turned. Other children's go-tos were a comfort blankie or a teddy, but not Noah. No, his was a skintight Mickey Mouse tee.

Granny Quealey, fed up with her grandson looking like a puny bodybuilder, suggested he let another little boy have a chance to enjoy the Mickey Mouse tee shirt. Noah had sniffed at this and told his granny the little boy should get his nana to take him on holiday to Disneyland so he could get his own Mickey Mouse shirt because he wasn't having his. Granny Quealey had joined him up to World Vision to sponsor a child quick smart, telling Roisin he needed to work on his empathy skills.

Noah, watching his mother all but sitting on her case, sighed as though he was dealing with an imbecile. 'And you'll break it if you do that.' He took a bite of the apple he held in his hand.

Roisin, who was wearing her trusty Mo-pants as she always did when doing pretty much everything bar work, clambered off the case. She sat back on her haunches, smoothed the dark curls plastered to her brow, and then glanced over at her son. She wanted to check that he hadn't suddenly morphed into his father because he'd sounded exactly like her ex-husband. Mercifully it wasn't Colin Quealey standing there but rather her little boy who was going through a know-it-all phase. At least Roisin hoped it was a phase and one he would soon grow out of. Colin hadn't. He was in his late thirties, and he was still a fecky know-it-all. She'd married a man who drove her potty playing the Trivial Pursuit. The thing was, Colin hadn't known it all, far from it, because if he had, he wouldn't have re-mortgaged their house behind her back, thus plunging them into financial chaos. His lies had sealed the fate of their flailing marriage.

'Ah, sure, I wish I had your talents there, son.' She focussed on Noah, glad of an excuse to take a break from her task and her mind off the bombshell Colin had dropped two weeks ago.

'What talents, Mummy? I do know a lot about gerbils. Is that what you mean? And I'm very good at spelling. Mrs Clancy says so. Remember she gave me a gold star for getting my three amp words, right? Damp, lamp and stamp. D.A.M.P—'

Roisin cut him off before he could go through his repertoire. 'You are a good speller, Noah, and you know a lot about gerbils, but that's not what I meant.'

'What then?' a little piece of apple shot from his mouth as he stared at her curiously.

'The talent to know everything there is to know in the world at the tender age of six. It's phenomenal. That's what I meant.'

Noah's eyes narrowed. He wasn't sure whether she meant what she was saying or whether she was being silly. Then, unable to work it out, he demanded, 'I'm nearly seven. How do you spell it?'

'What?'

'That big menal word.'

'You mean phenomenal?'

He nodded.

Roisin opened her mouth and closed it. The 'Ph' words had never been her strong point in spelling. Physics, physician, physique; they'd all had a big red cross next to them. She could add phenomenal to the list now. It was time to move the conversation on. 'And how's your packing coming along?' She asked in a complete change of subject.

'All done.'

'That was very quick. Did you follow the list I gave you?'

'Mummy, I'm not a baby. So I didn't need the list.'

'I see. Well, how about I come and have a look.'

Noah shrugged, clambering off the bed. Roisin followed him into his bedroom. The big blue monster from the film, *Monsters, Inc.* eyeballed them from a poster on the wall, and the duvet was covered with smaller versions. She noted the toys on the floor instead of in the toybox, and the open drawers, and sighed. The shiny *Monsters, Inc.* wheelie case, a Christmas gift from his nana, was standing at the foot of the bed, and she tossed it on the bed. It felt suspiciously light and, frowning, she unzipped it. The contents consisted of three pairs of underpants, three pairs of socks, a toothbrush and a *Monsters, Inc.* DVD.

'Noah, you've barely anything in here.'

'That's all I need, Mummy.'

'What about a jacket, your pyjamas?' Pyjamas was another word she couldn't spell to save herself. She recalled the subsequent big red cross next to the abbreviated version of PJs she'd run with on one particular test. Sister Joan hadn't been impressed with her thinking outside the box. 'And you'll need another couple of tee shirts, shorts, a pair of trousers and a sweater.' She was already pulling them out of the drawers and stuffing them in his case.

A horn sounded, and Roisin groaned. Colin couldn't be here already, could he? He was going out of his way to be helpful, insisting on driving them to Heathrow, never mind the traffic. She glanced at her wristwatch. He was early. Well, he would just have to wait.

'Daddy's here!' Noah picked up the gerbil cage and flung open the front door.

'Wait for me, Noah!' Roisin ordered from his bedroom.

The excitement in her son's voice made her throat constrict. Colin had promised to talk to him when they got back from Ireland. She had no clue how Noah would take his father's news. She did know things were changing, and there wasn't a single thing she could do about it. First things first, though, she needed to finish packing.

Chapter Two

Colin had completed three circuits of the block by the time Roisin, exhausted but victorious from her packing battle, appeared on the steps outside the tiny flat where she and Noah lived. She locked the door before bouncing their cases down the stairs behind her.

Noah, who was grinning out the passenger window of the backseat of his father's car, had paid no heed to his mother telling him to wait. She assumed Mr Nibbles and Steve were in there with him too. How Colin had convinced his mother to allow him to bring his son's gerbil family home with him was beyond her. Elsa Quealey had a long memory and was still haunted by finding Mr Nibbles nesting in her bra on a previous home visit. Perhaps in light of what Colin had divulged a fortnight ago, Elsa, too, was going out of her way to be helpful.

The boot of the second-hand BMW Colin drove these days popped open, and then Roisin's ex-husband clambered out from behind the wheel. He was red in the face, and his shirt and trousers were crumpled. If Roisin didn't know him, she'd have him pegged as a seedy car salesman instead of the suave financier he fancied himself. Elsa Quealey's home cooking had blessed him with a paunch too. He'd not had that when they were together, which didn't say much about Roisin's cooking.

Colin had never borne the heat well, either. It made him snappy like one of those little terrier dogs yapping at your heels. Still, this afternoon, he was all smiles as, leaving the car engine running, he swooped on her with a faux cheery, 'Roisin.'

Christ on a bike, was he going to kiss her on the cheek? Well, she was having none of it so, taking an instinctive step backwards, Roisin thrust her case at him, but not before she caught a whiff of the garlic remains of lunch on his breath.

Colin took the hint, clearing his throat as he gestured to the luggage and said, 'I've got these. You get in.'

She was glad to slide into the front seat and shut the door on a hot afternoon. 'I thought I told you to wait for me, Noah,' she admonished, twisting to glance back over her shoulder. He was buckled in, and the gerbils were scrabbling about in their cage on the seat next to him.

'You took too long.'

'Well, I wouldn't have if you'd packed according to the list I gave you. And that's beside the point. You're to listen when I tell you something. Are your ears painted on?' Jaysus wept. Had Mammy taken over her body just then? Roisin's hand settled on her chest in alarm. She'd better warn her sisters that, before long, they'd be saying things to their children like, 'take your coat off, or it'll be no use to you when you go outside' or, 'there's enough dirt in those ears to grow potatoes'.

Noah pouted.

The boot banged shut. Colin jumped in and glanced at Roisin, then Noah. 'Is everything alright?'

'I'm just after telling Noah he's to listen when I tell him something.'

'Good point.' Colin cleared his throat. 'You're to listen to your mother, Noah.'

Roisin side-eyed her ex. It wasn't often he backed her up. This fecky brown-nosing of his was unnerving, she thought, checking to see if Noah was computing what he'd been told. As it happened, he was listening to neither parent as he poked his finger in the gerbil cage for reasons known only to himself.

Colin pulled out into the traffic, and Roisin settled herself into her seat with a sigh. The car was stuffy despite the air con; she could smell old leather and an aftershave she didn't recognise. She gave a surreptitious sniff. Whatever it was didn't smell cheap, and in the close interior, its spicy notes were overpowering. Her finger strayed to the window button, and she pushed it, allowing it to slide down a crack. Then, digging her nails into her palm, she waited to see if Colin's fecky brown-nosing would go as far as leaving the window open when the air con was on. In days of old, he'd have closed it straight back up again.

It did! And Roisin managed to scrape up her manners. 'Thank you for picking us up, Colin. It would have been a nightmare squeezing onto the tube in this heat.' A glance at the harassed, hot pedestrians confirmed this. It was a beach day, not one to be trawling London's fumy streets.

'No problem. I would've had to have swung by to pick up Mr Nibbles and Steve anyway.'

'It's Stef, Daddy, and don't feed Mr Nibbles or Stef cabbage because it will give them runny poos.'

'Er, got it, Noah.'

As Colin braked suddenly, swearing under his breath at the motorcycle courier who'd pulled out right in front of him, Roisin's phone rang.

'That will be Nana, Daddy. She always rings when we're in the car. Mummy says she's got a sixth fecking sense.'

Roisin resolved to reign in her swearing, while Colin gripped the steering wheel a little tighter.

He momentarily forgot he was on his best behaviour. 'I remember.'

'Hello, Mammy,' Roisin answered. 'We're on our way to the airport now.'

'She's on her way to the airport now, Donal. Kiera put the chew toy down. That's Pooh's toy, so it is. Would you believe she's after having a tug-o-war with the poor dog? She's turned into a holy terror since she began toddling.'

A smile twitched as Roisin pictured the scene playing out in her mammy's living room. She watched a woman so busy tapping away at her phone she nearly walked into a lamppost as she waited for her mother to get to the point of her call. If indeed there was one, because more often than not, there wasn't.

'I'm ringing to tell you the plan.'

'If you mean the convoy to Claredonwotsit, you've already told me, and why do you sound like that?' Roisin said, remembering Moira's warning that Mammy was one step away from supplying them with walkie-talkies for their road trip. To use the iconic trucker phrase, 'Ten-four good buddy, over and out,' was on her ever-expanding bucket list, apparently.

'Like what?'

'Husky, like an Irish Al Pacino.'

'I woke up with a scratchy throat, and no, not that plan. The airport plan.'

'Ujjayi breathing could help with that, Mammy, and we don't need a plan. It's simple, so it is. Sure we've done it loads of times. Noah and

I get off the plane. We walk into the arrivals hall, you wave out, and then we head out to your car. Easy.'

'I'm quite happy breathing the way I am, thank you very much, Roisin. Donal, would you take the chew toy off Kiera before Moira turns up? She'll go mad if she sees her trying to hide it down her nappy. The little madam won the tug-o-war, Rosi, and it's not that simple because of the thousands of people arriving and departing Dublin airport at any given time. It's a busy international hub these days, you know.'

Roisin rolled her eyes. 'If you say so, Mammy.'

'I do. So, the plan is once you've located me, I'll be wearing my new linen BO blouse just so you know what to look out for. You've not seen it yet. It's gorgeous, and Ciara, with a C, says it takes ten years off me.'

'Is a BO blouse a particularly smelly blouse or something, Mammy?' Roisin was genuinely bewildered.

'Don't get smart with me, young lady. I've told you a million times BO is fashion speak for this season's hottest colour, burnt orange. It's in one ear and out the other with you, Rosi.'

Now that she mentioned it, that did ring a bell, Roisin thought, and it wasn't that things went in one ear and out the other. The problem was Mammy's ramblings were like white noise. She switched off, only switching back on to take note of the pertinent information. 'I'm with you now.'

'Glad to hear it. Right, so when we've made contact—'

'Mammy, you're picking me up at the airport, not playing the role of a Bond Girl in a BO blouse passing on top-secret information.'

'Don't keep interrupting me. I'm losing my train of thought. Where was I?'

'When we've made contact.'

'Yes, when we've made contact, I'll ring Donal on my mobile phone to tell him I have you both. He'll be waiting down the road, and once I give him the word, he'll drive down to the exit and collect us.'

'We could always send up a smoke signal or something instead,' Roisin suggested.

'That's the sort of remark I'd expect from Moira. It's a very good plan because the car parking at the airport is daylight robbery. I don't recall you putting your hand in your pocket on the many occasions I've picked you up from arrivals.'

That was true enough, Roisin thought, opting to say nothing.

'So, are you clear as to what's happening?'

'I am.'

'Grand. We'll see you soon. Would you tell Noah his nana and Poppa D can't wait to give him a big cuddle? But don't be giving that ex-husband of yours one.'

'I will and I won't. Bye for now, Mammy.'

'One more thing before you go, Roisin.'

'Mammy, why are you whispering like so?'

'I'm not,' Maureen whispered. 'Be quiet and listen, would yer. You're to keep an eye out for Daniel Day-Lewis at the airport. He could be on his way to America to make a film, or to attend an important meeting about a film in London, or the like. I might be spoken for, but that doesn't mean I've stopped wanting to pass on my congratulations for his outstanding performance as one of your Mohican fellas.'

Roisin smirked. Most people would commend the man for his acting skills in *My Left Foot* or *The Boxer*, but not her mammy. Oh no, she'd give him a pat on the back for running through the forest in a loin cloth. 'Alright, Mammy, will do. I'll be seeing you soon. Bye now.' She returned the phone to her bag and felt Colin glance her way as he came to a halt at the lights.

'How's Maureen keeping?'

'Grand. Never been better, in fact. She's happy with Donal in their new home with the sea view in Howth.'

'That's good. I wish my mother would meet someone.'

That was a frightening thought, but Colin was thinking out loud, and she was spared from answering as he moved on to ask how Moira and Aisling were.

'Oh, they're busy, you know, with the babies and helping their fellas train for the marathon later this year.'

'Boston?' Colin looked interested.

'Dublin.'

'Oh.' The car crawled along to the next set of lights, and they sat in silence until Colin spoke again. 'And how's Pat? Is he still with his actress girlfriend? Will he be flying in for this reunion weekend?'

'Cindy, and she's his fiancée now. They got engaged recently. No, they're not coming over because they've too many work commitments, or at least that's what Patrick said.' A convenient excuse, in her opinion.

'Engaged!' Colin drummed his fingers on the steering wheel. 'Well, I never thought I'd see the day Patrick O'Mara decided to tie the knot. She must be something special.'

'She's got enormous boobs,' Noah piped up. 'Mum says they're like two overblown balloons attached to her chest.'

'Noah!' It was true, though. And she supposed Patrick had been pegged the eternal playboy until Cindy had changed all that. She'd forgotten how well Colin used to get on with Patrick, but why shouldn't they? They had loads in common, like both being arses. 'Yes, she's good as family, already calling Mammy "Mom" and all that. They're talking about getting married next summer on a Greek Island.' She didn't want to get into how that had been received by her future sister-in-law's future Mammy-in-law and stifling a yawn, she closed her eyes, leaning back into the headrest. She hoped Colin would take the hint and stop prattling on about Pat.

Her thoughts drifted to her nieces and nephew. She could see more and more of her son in his cousin Kiera as the months passed. She had that same mischievous twinkle in her eyes. What would Aoife and Kieran be like?

Lately, Roisin had been feeling a powerful tug toward home. Of course, this was down to the arrival of the twins because she didn't want to miss a thing, and they changed almost daily when they were babies. Look at Kiera, she had a new trick each time she saw her, and now she was even toddling. Moira kept her filled in on her daughter's antics right enough, but it wasn't the same as seeing them for herself. She'd never thought she'd be the long-distance aunt who appeared every few months bearing gifts. Actually, scrap that. She was bearing no gifts this time around. There wasn't room in the wheelie case.

Then there was Shay. They'd been together for nearly two years, and while she was barely hanging onto her thirties, he'd only enter his later this year. He was brilliant with Noah, but they'd never talked about whether he wanted his own children. Maybe this was because, living in separate countries, him in Ireland and her in England, their relationship had somehow never progressed to cosy domesticity. The times they saw each other were too precious for knuckling down to the nitty gritty of moving their relationship to the next level. Or maybe she was frightened of what the answer would be given the nearly ten-year age gap between them.

She didn't have the luxury of procrastination and, lately, babies had been on her mind. She didn't know whether this was down to her beautiful new nieces and nephew or if her biological clock was having a last hurrah. She did know how she felt about Shay and he about her, but they'd never had a serious conversation about where they were headed. He'd said it was one of the things he loved about her. Her easy-going nature. But a woman nudging forty and having thoughts about babies couldn't afford to be laid-back, even she knew that.

A melancholy stole over her, and she rested her hands on her belly, opened her mouth wide and inhaled. This was her favourite yoga mood-elevating breathing technique. So what if Colin wondered what she was up to with her jaw hanging open.

'Daddy, that's Mummy's yoga breathing. She does it in the car, only with her eyes open while driving. Sometimes people stare at her when she's stopped because the light is red, but she doesn't care, and I just wave at them.'

Roisin wasn't listening. She was thinking about Shay. She wished it was him she was looking out for at the airport instead of Mammy in her BO blouse, but she'd have to wait till his appearance in Claredonwotsit on Saturday afternoon. Their sporadic get-togethers always ensured enthusiastic riding sessions, but it was getting harder and harder to say goodbye. She sighed. Perhaps all the fresh country air would help her gain some perspective of where she/they were at.

A shift was beginning to happen inside her that signalled Colin might not be the only one for whom change was coming.

Chapter Three

♥

Two weeks earlier

Roisin automatically picked up the bottle of Dolce & Gabbana's Light Blue Eau de Toilette. Shay had given it to her for her birthday, and she was about to spray it when she paused. It wasn't Shay she was heading out to dinner with. Colin would pick her up in twenty minutes, and he didn't warrant dousing herself in her favourite perfume.

She put the bottle down and stepped back from the dressing table to eye her shift dress in the mirror. Nothing suggestive there, she thought, turning from side to side. But then, eyeing the neckline, she panicked. Would she be flashing too much cleavage when she leaned over to eat her meal? To reassure herself, she bent forward, miming using a knife and fork and was relieved to see there was nothing on show that would send her ex-husband mad with lust over his main.

The makeup she'd applied was minimal, and she'd scraped her dark hair back in a low ponytail. Colin had always preferred her to wear her hair down. He also liked her in heels, and Roisin had never been a heels sort of girl; unlike Aisling and Moira, she only owned one pair for special occasions. Tonight was not a special occasion, as mysterious as it was. Hence, the flat sandals she'd picked out.

For the hundredth time since Colin had telephoned her earlier in the week to see if she was free on Thursday night, she wondered what he felt he had to tell her in person. Her stomach had been in knots because, for a moment, she'd thought he would suggest meeting up at the Italian place they'd always gone to for birthdays and anniversaries. She hadn't stepped foot in the place since they split up and couldn't have borne a trip down memory lane. Instead, it was a new place called Vine he'd mentioned trying to book them a table at.

If she had to make a stab at what he was planning to divulge, she'd roll with him having a girlfriend at long last. One whom he wanted to introduce to Noah and, out of courtesy (and character), he'd decided to let her know his intentions first. If this was the case, he deserved a round of applause. The fact he was broke and living at home with his domineering mother hadn't seen London's single women battering down his door since he and Roisin had split. Good luck to him, she thought, because while there was no love lost between them, the anger and hurt of his deception had long since faded, and these days her feelings toward him were ambivalent. So long as his lady friend treated Noah with kindness and didn't try to step on her toes by mothering him, she couldn't care less if he had a girlfriend.

How Noah would take the news of his father having a new woman in his life didn't worry Roisin. He was easily bought, their son, and he'd be perfectly happy about whomever his dad spent time with so long as there was ice cream and McDonald's fries in it for him.

Colin had rung her back the next day to say he'd secured a table at the restaurant he'd mentioned and that he'd pick up her and Noah at six thirty on Thursday evening. Another clue, Roisin had thought, because Friday night would be reserved for the girlfriend. Noah was to go to his granny's for his tea. It had been on the tip of Roisin's tongue to check she wasn't expected to go Dutch for dinner, not with her ex-husband's champagne tastes on beer money. Oh no, this meal was his idea. He could spring for it. Instead, she'd asked what sort of food Vine served and had received the reply it was fine dining. To Roisin's mind, this meant she'd be making herself a sandwich when she got home later to fill the gap left by the teensy-tiny servings of food.

Colin had been quick to add he'd had to pull a few strings to secure a table at London's latest hip eatery, given it was booked out months in advance. That's where they'd always been different. To be seen in the right places mattered to him, whereas Roisin wouldn't have cared if it was the local Wimpy they were going to. At least then she could have worn her trusty Mo-pants and been done with it.

Her eyes flitted to the yoga pants rebranded by her mammy balled up on her bedroom floor. It was a bonus that Mammy was too busy with Kiera, Aoife and Kieran these days to keep harping on about unleashing a maternity Mo-pant on the unsuspecting Irish public. The London market stall where Roisin picked up the yoga pants on the cheap before carting them over to Dublin for Mammy to rename and mark-up didn't run to maternity. Although they did run to bloating. Roisin could attest to that.

Sometimes it made her sad to think of Noah missing out on the quality time with his nana his cousins would take for granted because they lived closer. Not sad enough to invite Mammy and Donal to stay, obviously – her flat was far too small for that – but sad all the same. The three cousins would form a tight bond, too, spending their formative years in such close quarters. Moira, Tom and Kiera would continue to live in the family apartment over O'Mara's with Aisling, Quinn and the twins for at least another year or two. She sighed. The best she could hope for was for Noah to be the cool 'London' cousin who came to visit.

Of course, none of this bothered Noah. He was excited about seeing his cousins in a fortnight, but Roisin knew the excitement would wear off once he realised the twins, at just over two months, weren't up to much. Although she suspected he'd get a lot of mileage out of their mustard-coloured poo. He was also fascinated with his Aunty Aisling, or rather Aunty Aisling's breasts. On their last visit, seeing her breastfeeding the twins, he'd likened her to the cow being milked on a school farm trip. Aisling had been too delirious to mind. At least Kiera was of more interest to him now that she was toddling and beginning to demonstrate a wilful streak. Mammy, in particular, was enjoying her eldest granddaughter's newfound assertiveness. This was because she'd shouted at Moira more than once over her formative years, 'I hope someday you have children just like you.'

Roisin picked up her purse and stalked out to the living room to await Colin's arrival. Noah was seated cross-legged, the gerbil cage on the carpet in front of him. He was amid an earnest chat with Mr Nibbles and Steve or Stef about how he was going to his granny's for his tea, which meant he wouldn't have to eat yucky things like broccoli.

The rodent couple stopped nibbling the lettuce he'd stuffed into the cage to listen. Neither gerbil had suffered from empty-nest syndrome since their babies had been farmed out to family, friends, and a local pet shop. That was a blessing. Nor would they be blessed with more babby gerbils because she'd put her foot down, insisting it was Colin's responsibility to ensure this didn't happen again. He was the one who'd bought Mr Nibbles in the first instance, and it would be up to him to rear any future gerbil offspring. This, in turn, had seen his mother threaten him with eviction should he bring any gerbils home to live with them. So Mr Nibbles had been neutered. Still, it didn't stop him from sitting on poor Steve-Stef, and Roisin supposed he was reliving past glories.

Colin had said he'd pick them up at six thirty sharp and he was nothing if not punctual. It was now twenty minutes past six. As she sank into the sofa, a spring poked into the back of her thigh. A new sofa wasn't high on her list of priorities, however. Not now she was a qualified yoga instructor and her heart was set on the yoga studio she'd made her mind up to open when she'd saved enough money. This meant any extra cash, like the bonus Norman, her boss, had given her at Christmas, was squirrelled away. Poor Norman had lucked out when she'd been employed as his secretary. She was rubbish at her job, so the bonus really had been unexpected. Roisin twiddled her thumbs, willing six thirty to roll around so Colin could put her out of her misery and get whatever he had to say off his chest.

The telephone ringing was a welcome diversion, and rather than race her son to the phone as she was apt to do, she let him scramble to his feet and answer it.

'Hello, Noah Quealey, speaking.' A second later, he said, 'Hello, Aunty Moira,' and then, taking a deep breath, filled his aunt in on his day at school. There was a brief silence before he informed her too much cabbage would give Kiera's pet gerbil, Demi, runny poo.

Roisin winced as he divulged mummy wouldn't be able to talk to her for long because Daddy was picking them up. He would have his tea at Granny's while Mummy and Daddy went to a restaurant.

She was for it now, Roisin thought as her son rounded up his side of the conversation.

'I don't mind not going with them because Mummy said she'll need binoculars to see the food on her plate, and I'm hungry. Fish finger and chips hungry. Not vegetable hungry.'

Roisin slunk low on the sofa. The last thing she felt like was a grilling from Moira as to why she was dining with her ex-husband or, as Moira would no doubt word it, 'that chinless feck'. Besides, there was nothing she could tell her given she didn't know what had prompted Colin to organise tonight, only that he'd been insistent she come. A quick check of her wristwatch revealed it was now six twenty-five. Five minutes until Colin's horn would sound as he idled on the street outside since short-term parking was a near impossibility.

Noah thrust the phone at his mother. 'Aunty Moira wants to speak to you.'

Roisin pressed it to her ear. 'I'm going out in a minute or two. What do you want, Moira?'

'Why are you going out all cosy like with that chinless feck you used to be married to?'

Yes, Roisin thought grimly, it was as she'd predicted. 'There's nothing cosy about it. He's got something he wants to talk to me about, that's all.'

'Jaysus wept, Rosi, wait until Mammy hears about this.'

'She'll only hear about it if you tell her.'

'It's my duty as her youngest child to keep her in the loop.'

'Feck off, Moira.'

'Listen, Rosi,' Moira's voice was deadly serious now. 'You're to promise me, cross your heart hope to die, that you will not have one wine too many and let him sweet talk you into going for a ride for old time's sake.'

'Moira.' Roisin was indignant. 'In case you haven't noticed, I'm happily involved with Shay.'

'Ah, Rosi, but you know what you're like.'

'What do you mean by that?'

'Fickle. And there was another reason we called you easy osi Rosi, you know.'

For the second time in their short conversation, Roisin told her sister what she could do. 'I am not easy osi Rosi, thanks very much. I've been very assertive since the divorce, and I know my own mind. Besides, Colin has moved on too. Literally, I think. I'm guessing that's what this evening is in aid of.' She didn't want to say any more with big ears flapping nearby. 'That's him now. I've got to go,' she lied. There were still three minutes to go.

'Ring me as soon as you get home, because I'll not be able to concentrate on Bally K until I know what's going on with yer both, neither will Ash, or Mammy for that matter.'

'Nothing is going on! Goodbye.' Roisin pressed the button ending the call, and smiled sweetly at Noah. 'All set? Daddy will be here any minute.'

Forty minutes later, Roisin was seated at a beautifully laid table with the silverware gleaming against the expanse of white cloth. She was staring down at the meanest sliver of smoked salmon laid upon a swirl of horseradish puree and garnished with curls of green scallion. The finishing touch to the entrée was the artistic speckles of lemon zest decorating the rim of the enormous white plate, the size of which dwarfed the blob which wouldn't fill an ant.

Colin was prattling on about Michelin stars as he made short work of his scallop on pea puree. Roisin looked up in time to see a salad sprig disappearing in his mouth. He reminded her of a water buffalo eating grass. So far, they'd danced around the edges of why they were here, with Colin making polite enquiries after her work and family. By the time their waiter for the evening, Jean-Claude, had flapped open a napkin to drape over her lap, she was ready for him to launch onto the weather.

Jean-Claude needn't have worried about the napkin, Roisin thought as he presented her with the entrée she'd ordered a short while later. There'd not be a crumb escaping from her mouth, and she regretted not having had a sandwich before she left home. There'd been further distraction when Colin made a show of ordering the wine by doing that awful swirly spitty thing he always did before settling on a French white. To be fair, it was delicious, she'd give him that. Her ex-husband knew his wines. And if he kept topping her glass like so and if her main was no bigger than her entrée, there was a chance she'd morph into her drunken alter ego, Agnetha. She'd be singing ABBA at the top of her lungs by the time they left the restaurant.

She wolfed down her salmon sliver in one fell swoop, then looked at Colin with her eyebrow raised in expectation of what he wanted to say. Instead, he waved at someone he knew and then, picking up his napkin, dabbed at his mouth. Roisin's nerves began to jangle as he got on them. She wanted to reach across the table, grab him by the lapels and tell him to spit out whatever it was. Then again, there'd been enough spitting with the wine. How on earth had she slept next to this man for all those years? He was just so... so... so annoying.

'The thing is, Roisin,' he said at last, sounding out her name formally.

She cocked her head to the right, indicating she was all ears as she waited for him to tell her he'd met someone.

'An opportunity has come my way that's too good to miss. I've been offered a job. A rather good job, actually.'

This wasn't what she'd expected, and a frown puckered the space between her brows because she sensed a 'but' coming.

'But it's in Dubai.'

'What suburb of London is that in?'

'Em, Dubai in the Arab Emirates, Roisin.'

She did know that on some level but couldn't understand how he'd continue having Noah every second weekend. She said as much. 'Dubai to London's a long way to come once a fortnight.'

'That's the thing. Our current arrangement will have to change. But, of course, Mother's only too happy for Noah to stay with her every second weekend.' Colin cleared his throat and began fiddling with his spoon, unable to meet her gaze. 'To be honest, she's petrified she'll hardly see Noah once I go.'

This sounded like a foregone conclusion, Roisin thought, batting his comment away. She nearly swatted Jean-Claude as he moved in to ask how they were enjoying their food, but catching sight of Roisin's face, he thought better of it and backed away slowly. Colin wasn't asking for her opinion as to whether he should accept a position in Dubai. Instead, he was telling her this was what he was doing. She was dimly aware of him whining like a mosquito about how he'd hit rock bottom when they'd lost the house, and he'd had to move in with his mother, blah-blah-blah. And all she could think was, where was Noah in all of this?

'Noah loves his granny, but you're his father, Colin,' she finally interrupted, having heard enough.

'I'm aware of that, Roisin, but listen because opportunities, and well, to be frank, salaries like this don't get dangled very often. In the long run, it's best for Noah. He won't have to miss out.'

'But he will miss out, Colin. He'll miss out on you,' Roisin added lamely. Colin Quealey was, in summary, an arse, but he was also her son's father, and while he would never be in the running for Dad of the Year, he was the only father Noah had.

Colin began waffling about how he'd fly home every few months. Perhaps Roisin could bring Noah to Dubai for a holiday at some point, or he could travel with his granny and come in the school holidays for a fortnight. Roisin couldn't fathom Noah being away from her for a fortnight, let alone in a foreign country.

She held up her hand to interrupt her ex-husband halfway through his speech. 'You're going to have to tell Noah yourself, Colin.'

His assurances that Noah would adjust to their new arrangement in no time faltered. 'I thought it might be best if we told him together.'

Roisin knew what that meant. She'd tell Noah his father was moving to another country, but it was all good because it meant Noah could have whatever he wanted. Oh, and the odd holiday to Dubai, too, while Colin nodded enthusiastically behind her.

Well, it wasn't happening. This wasn't on her. 'No,' she said flatly. And putting her napkin on the table, she pushed her seat back and got up. She'd get the tube home. But first, she'd call in at the chippy.

Chapter Four

The airport pick-up ran to plan. To be fair, it wouldn't have mattered whether Mammy was wearing the BO blouse or not. She was hard to miss jumping up and down, rasping, 'Rosi, Noah! Over here.'

Her voice reminded Roisin of a spectre with a bony hand reaching out from the grave toward them. That or Marianne Faithful driving through Paris in a sports car. Noah, too, was wary, and Roisin had to tug him along to meet the creature bopping about masquerading as his nana.

Mammy was sickening for something alright, Roisin thought. Whatever she was coming down with, she hoped she didn't pass it on. Heading back to London on Sunday night with laryngitis wasn't part of her plan. She knew Norman wouldn't be impressed if she had to take more time off. As she strode toward her Mammy, Roisin observed her scanning the hall furtively as if she were an FBI agent hunting a suspect.

Roisin knew precisely who she was trying to track down and decided to pip her at the post as they pushed past a milling family of four and stepped into her line of sight. 'Before you ask Mammy, we didn't spot Daniel on his way to make a new film.'

'And hello to you too, Roisin. Sure, that's no way to greet your mammy,' Maureen replied huskily, and then her expression went from excited at seeing her eldest daughter and grandson to a brow-furrowed frown as she added, 'And what's this Daniel business? You're very pally-wally there with the man, being on a first-name basis. It's Mr Day-Lewis to you, my girl. Show some respect, Roisin. The man won an orange orb award.'

'Golden Globe, Mammy, and we've not seen Mr Day-Lewis.' Roisin stood corrected.

Maureen pulled her and Noah into a welcoming Arpège-scented hug then, releasing them, she pulled her mobile from her bag.

Roisin was relieved that, for once, Mammy didn't shout into her phone as Donal was informed they were ready to be collected.

'Why do you sound like that, Nana?' Noah eyed the woman who looked and smelled like his nana cautiously.

'Well, now, I'd tell you it was down to a sore throat, Noah, but your nana can't afford to lose her voice. No. Not when yer Great, Great Aunt Noreen's after making a special request for Donal and me to sing "Islands in the Stream" at the reunion party. So I'm saying it's just a little tickle, is all. I'm using the power of positive thinking to will it away like the man I saw in the late-night television adverts. And, just so you know, I'll rest my voice for the next wee while.' Maureen tucked her phone away and mimed, zipping her lips shut before holding her hand out for her grandson to take.

Noah weighed up this answer and, coming to the conclusion that it didn't make much sense, decided it was safe to hold his nana's hand because she wasn't an imposter.

Then, her attention turned to Roisin. 'Who'd have thought Noreen would be a Kenny and Dolly fan? You know you learn something new about a person every day, so you do.'

Roisin, smirked at Mammy, who was oblivious to having just wheezed out at least fifty words. So much for resting her voice! 'I'd have thought you'd have been better doing a "Bette Davis Eyes" rendition,' she said. It was just as well Shay would be on hand with his fiddle to help liven up Donal's performance if he had to make a solo appearance.

'Roisin, would you use the brains God gifted you. That's hardly a duet, now is it? What's Donal supposed to do with himself while I'm going on about yer Bette Davis wan?'

'I don't know.' Roisin shrugged. 'Play the tin whistle?'

Maureen shot her a withering look, and then her expression changed as fast as the weather on a summer's day in Ireland. 'C'mon now. Donal has an expected ETA of five minutes past four.'

'Ten-four, little buddy,' Roisin muttered, bringing up the rear as they headed toward the exit.

Maureen swung her gaze to Roisin. 'I'd tell you not to be a smart arse, Roisin, but I'm not saying a word.' She narrowly avoided walking into the glass doors because of their slight delay in sliding open.

The hustle and bustle of people wanting to get to their destination, horns sounding, and the reek of car fumes and cigarette smoke greeted them outside. The early evening air was unexpectedly warm, and Roisin shrugged out of the light jacket she'd thrown on over her tee shirt.

'Don't be making eye contact now,' Maureen hissed.

'What was that, Mammy?' Roisin tossed her jacket over her arm, dipping her head toward her mammy, unable to make out what she was saying over the general din.

'I said don't be making eye contact.'

'With whom?' Jaysus wept. She sounded more and more like Darth Vadar with each passing moment, Roisin thought.

'Yer taxi men, of course. Look at them there all hopeful like.'

Roisin glanced at the lined-up taxis, and her eyes locked briefly with a driver whose expression was doleful. She was tempted to clamber in and ask for a return trip to the Ring of Kerry to cheer him up.

Maureen knew her daughter well enough to put a restraining hand on her forearm, her hard stare conveying the message. 'Don't even think about it, Roisin.'

'Nana, what colour car will Poppa D be in?'

'A blue one.'

'What?'

A car was tooting ahead, and a woman pushing a luggage trolley hurried toward it.

'*Pardon*, Noah. And Nana said a blue car.'

'Like that one, Nana?' He pointed to a car crawling into the zone behind a shuttle bus.

Maureen nodded vigorously and ruffled his hair.

What happened next took Roisin unawares. A sense of deja vu as Donal drew up and beeped his horn, waving out excitedly, sucker punched her. She loosened the neck of her tee shirt, feeling as though it were strangling her. She'd been here so many times before, only instead of Donal pulling up to collect them, it used to be her daddy. Her chest constricted as the emotions took her by surprise. The rawness of him no longer being with them had long since softened, but the knowledge he was gone would hit her afresh. On those occasions, it would lodge in her throat, and she'd have to swallow hard, replacing sadness with happy memories of which there were truckloads. 'I miss you, Daddy,' she said to herself.

'Move it, Roisin.'

Maureen's rasp pulled her out of her reverie as she was pushed toward the car. A curly head appeared out the passenger window.

AN O'MARA'S REUNION 31

'Pooh!' Noah cried, charging toward the poodle.

Pooh was equally as rapturous, and once the boy-dog reunion was over, Donal, who'd left the car engine running, greeted Noah with a man-to-man handshake. It morphed into a bear hug, and then it was Roisin's turn.

The lovely thing about her mammy's live-in man-friend, Roisin thought, feeling his solidness, was he understood how she felt. How they all felt. If she were to relay what she had just experienced to him, he'd hug her all the tighter. It was one of the things that made Donal, a widower himself, perfect for her mammy. That and his bottomless pit of patience, of course, she thought as he let her go and opened the car boot.

'I'll see to these,' he said, picking up her wheelie case. 'You and Noah hop on in. There's a poodle desperate to see you both.'

Mother and son squished in with Pooh in the middle, and Roisin greeted the dog affectionately, scratching behind his ear. He woofed joyfully. In the background, country music crooned.

'Shush now, Pooh. Donal's got to concentrate,' Maureen croaked from the front passenger seat as she turned down the radio's volume and retrieved a Fisherman's Friend lozenge packet from the glove box.

'Don't you feel vulnerable with him breathing down your neck like so?' Roisin asked Donal as he settled in behind the wheel. Pooh made no secret of his green streak when it came to Donal. He saw him as a rival for Mammy's affection.

'Not at all, Roisin. Sure, we've a secret weapon which has put a stop to the ear-lobe nipping, haven't we, Mo? And that voice of yours is getting worse.'

Maureen nodded her agreement that it was and then reached down to retrieve a bright-yellow flip-flop, which she dangled in front of

Pooh. There was a yip-yap of excitement before he took it in his mouth, and then a sigh of contentment followed by silence.

'I give Maureen full credit for the idea,' Donal said, smiling at his beloved.

'Eyes on the road, Donal,' Maureen's voice might be fading, but she seemed to grow taller in her seat. Then, she twisted to look past Pooh to where Roisin was wedged against the door behind Donal. 'Rosi, it was a simple fix. I realised the flip-flop is to Pooh what a dummy is to a newborn. Once I'd bought him a pair, he left Donal's alone. Of course, the babby Kiera wasn't happy, so I had to get her a pair too. I chose pink ones, but then Moira was after giving out about stereotypes and whatnot, so I bought a green pair instead. I've been using the pink ones, so it all worked out. Kiera and Pooh have made peace since they each have their own flip-flops to play with.'

Donal angled the car into the traffic flow. 'Rest your voice now, Mo.'

Maureen began stuffing in the Fisherman's Friends lozenges. Donal picked up where she left off, keeping up a steady stream of chatter while she sucked her lozenge furiously. The packet was passed over the back to Noah's request, and he popped one in his mouth only to pull a face and slip it into the seat pocket in front of him. A few minutes later, as they passed Ballymun, Maureen was already on her third cough sweet.

'Mammy eating a whole packet won't cure your sore throat,' Roisin said, leaning forward in her seat. 'You'll have a sore throat and mouth ulcers to boot.'

Maureen didn't respond, helping herself to a fourth strong-smelling lozenge.

To be fair, she did sound better when she spoke up, Roisin thought five minutes later. Should she contact the Guinness Book of Records, perhaps, because she couldn't recall her mammy ever having been silent that long? Wonders never ceased.

'I just remembered what I meant to tell you, Rosi.'

'Are you sure you wouldn't rather just write it down, Mo?' Donal asked, concern creasing his craggy features.

'No, I'll be grand, Donal.' Maureen's voice was like sandpaper scraping as she directed what she said next at Roisin. 'Your second cousin Glen's after replying to Noreen's invitation to say he'll be coming to the reunion. None of us has seen him in years. Not since he moved to London with his father, Hugh, when he was ten. Hugh passed away several years ago, and Glen has been living in Dubai of all places, but sure, technology is marvellous because your cousin Finbar had an email address for Glen. Would you believe it?' She didn't pause to see if Roisin did believe it. 'Noreen said she nearly fell off her chair when Emer presented her with an email from him to say he was looking forward to seeing us all. You and he got along great guns when you were young. Do you remember, Roisin? You, Patrick and your sisters stayed with Glen in Hugh and Dara's big house in Killybun a few times in the summer holidays.'

Roisin thought it strange that Colin should be going to Dubai and Glen coming back. She conjured up an image of a tow-headed nine-year-old boy who'd been her partner in crime during family parties. She smiled, remembering how it had been her job to distract her mammy away from the plate of Jaffa cakes so Glen could whip it off the table and stash it in the dumbwaiter. Then they'd pull it upstairs to the family apartment and have a feast that made them feel sick. Patrick, tell-tale-tit he was, had told on them, earning them both a clip around the ear, but it had been worth it. She also had a vague memory of playing you show me yours, I'll show you mine with cousin Glen when she was six or so, not that she'd be telling Mammy that. And, of course, she remembered those holidays at the big house in Killybun. Aunt Dara had left them to their own devices, and they'd roamed the nearby fields, having a grand old time blackberrying and building huts from dusk to dawn.

Mammy was still talking, Roisin realised, wondering how life had worked out for Glen. Roisin had hazy memories of something happening with his mam to cause his dad to move them to London but couldn't remember what it was. Was he married now with children? she pondered. Or divorced like herself? It was so hard to picture a grown-up version of him.

'Terrible sad it was what happened,' Maureen said, and her hair swished back and forth as she shook her head at the memories.

'What was?' Donal asked, his interest piqued as he forgot about her resting her voice.

'Hugh was Brian's cousin, and Dara, Hugh's wife, packed her bags one day, leaving a note to say she was off to Canada to look after her poorly sister. She left Hugh and Glen to fend for themselves. The poor lad was only nine when his mammy left. Hugh received a letter a few months later saying she wouldn't be back. There was no return address on the envelope and, not long after, Hugh sold up and moved himself and Glen to London for a fresh start. He remarried a few years later, but by then I think the damage was done for poor Glen because Noreen told me yesterday he's never married. I don't suppose he can find it in himself to trust a woman after what his mammy did. In my opinion, give a girl a boy's name like Dara, and you're asking for trouble, mind.'

'Mammy, did no one ever hear from Dara again?'

'Not a soul.'

'So, you only had Uncle Hugh's word that she'd gone to Canada?' Roisin was aghast. 'He could have murdered her and buried her in the back garden for all you know. Did none of you think to follow up on what he said?'

'Sure, Roisin, where do you get an idea like that?' Maureen bristled, summoning up the remains of her voice to say, 'Why would we? Hugh wouldn't do anything untoward. He wasn't the type. For one thing, he was a solicitor and don't you remember that big house they lived in, Killybun?'

'So let me get this straight. According to you, solicitors and people who live in big houses can't be murderers? Is that what you're saying, Mammy?'

Maureen feigned muteness.

Roisin supposed Dara's family would have made noise if they'd never seen or heard from her again. She mulled over what Mammy had just relayed. To leave one's husband was something she could relate to. It happened. People made mistakes, but to abandon your child without a word like Glen's mammy had done was unfathomable. She pondered what could have made her do it, trying to pull up a memory of Dara O'Mara. All she could come up with was a pale, quiet woman with arresting dark eyes like her son's. She had no clue where Mammy got the idea Dara's name was a factor in her running off.

'The poor lad,' Donal said, braking for the lights.

Roisin silently agreed. It had all come back to her now. She remembered how as a child, she'd not been privy to the ins and outs of why Aunt Dara no longer lived at home with her Uncle Hugh and favourite cousin. All she'd known was there'd be no more holidays to Killybun. Uncle Hugh and Glen left for England not long after that. She'd not seen either of them again. From an adult perspective, she could only imagine how confusing it must have been to Glen at the time because he lost his mam and the house he'd always called home.

Roisin was too busy thinking through all of this to notice Noah's face had lost its rosy glow.

'Mummy, you wouldn't leave me, Mr Nibbles and Stef, would you?'

Roisin peered around Pooh. 'Of course I wouldn't. Never.'

'Not even when we drive you mad?'

Roisin resolved to stop using that particular turn of phrase. 'Never, do you hear me?' She realised she'd just committed to Mr Nibbles and Steve-Stef for life.

'Never,' Maureen reiterated, tapping the side of her head. 'She can't have been well up here, Noah.'

Roisin put Glen out of her mind. She'd be seeing him soon enough.

Chapter Five

Roisin beamed, seeing Bronagh had stayed late to greet her and Noah as they burst into O'Mara's reception after a slow crawl into the city. Rush hour in Dublin was always a nightmare, and had been made worse by Pooh. The poodle, fed up with the flip-flop, decided to have a nap, twisting about in the seat until he was sprawled across herself and Noah. She'd drawn the short or arse end – however you wanted to look at it.

Donal had turned to Maureen and said, 'I told you not to give him the doggy treats at lunchtime.'

Despite Pooh's best efforts, they'd survived the journey, tumbling from the car once Donal pulled up outside the guesthouse. Donal waved Roisin in, saying he'd see to her case.

The reception area, aside from Bronagh and Freya, was deserted and smelled of the glorious Oriental lilies in full bloom in the vase on the front desk. Roisin smiled, holding back as Noah received a welcome fit for a king from their long-serving staff member while Freya hung back awkwardly.

'Have you room for a custard cream before your dinner?' Bronagh lowered her voice conspiratorially and winked at Roisin over the top of her son's head.

Noah's face lit up, and he informed the receptionist he had plenty of room. He liked custard creams and loved coming to O'Mara's because Bronagh and Mrs Flaherty always spoiled him rotten. It had saddened him to learn he wouldn't see O'Mara's breakfast cook this time round for his customary bacon butty. Still, Nana had assured him she'd fry him bacon for his breakfast tomorrow. In the meantime, the custard creams were decent compensation.

'You know where they are. Help yourself.' Bronagh nudged him toward the reception desk, where she kept her not-so-secret stash of biscuits in the drawer.

As her son trotted over to help himself, Roisin launched herself on the woman who was as much a part of the O'Mara family as any of them. She was also the luckiest, given she wasn't expected to attend tomorrow's reunion. Nevertheless, Roisin was curious to see Glen again and discover what life was like for him in Dubai. She thought you never lost the fondness for friends or, in his case, the family you got on well with when you were small.

Bronagh gave Roisin a tight squeeze in return. Then she released her to hold her at arm's-length as she gave her the once over. 'You're looking very well, Roisin. I like your hair. It's longer than when I last saw you. Mind, it always did grow like wildfire. And if you don't mind me saying so, you're a little on the skinny side. Are you eating properly?'

'I eat very well, Bronagh.' Roisin tried to anyway, but life was busy, and the odd night of beans or spaghetti on toast never harmed anyone. You'd think it had been years since she'd last seen her instead of last month, Roisin thought with a grin.

'Hmm, I suppose it's down to the yoga.' Bronagh glanced down at her own middle. 'I might have to give it a go.'

'You've been saying that forever, Bronagh. And you're looking very well yourself.'

Over the older woman's shoulder, Roisin spied Freya, still loitering shyly. They'd only met briefly when she'd last been over for the arrival of the twins. Roisin smiled warmly at her, knowing it had been a rocky start for the night receptionist, who was studying hospitality management at the Dublin Institute of Technology. All that was water under the bridge now, though, because with Aisling's time stretched thin juggling O'Mara's and being a mammy, Freya was proving herself a godsend.

Roisin had been informed by Donal at Mammy's behest on the drive here of tomorrow's plan. Freya, who'd got the job as O'Mara's night receptionist because of her family connections, was Great Aunt Noreen's grand-niece. She would squeeze into the back of Aisling and Quinn's car and could keep an eye on the twins for the journey southwest. She was very helpful when it came to the babies, by all accounts. This had given Roisin pause. She'd like to be helpful too, but aside from being a sounding board for a worn-out Aisling, there wasn't much she could do from London. Her role tomorrow would be to keep Kiera company in Moira and Tom's car, so she'd have to brush up on her nursery rhymes and whatnot. Meanwhile, Noah would stay with his Nana and Poppa D tonight for one-on-one grandparent time and travel down to Claredoncally with them in the morning. As for Pooh, he was going on a holiday himself. Mammy's friend, Rosemary Farrell, had offered to have him for the weekend. Donal said the poodle had been excited over the prospect and would be grand so long as Rosemary didn't try to part him from the flip-flops Maureen had bought him.

A shout of laughter from a passer-by sounded as the door to the guesthouse opened, and Maureen and Donal trundled in. Donal pulled Roisin's wheelie case behind him while Maureen gripped Pooh's lead as he pranced alongside her.

'Hello there,' Bronagh sang out, attempting and failing to stride toward the poodle to give him the scratch behind the ears she knew he enjoyed. But, unfortunately, her pencil skirt did not allow for anything other than mincing.

Maureen opened her mouth to greet Bronagh and Freya in return, but a whisper was the only sound forthcoming. Her voice had finally given up the ghost as they'd reached the quays on their way here. It gave her no choice but to locate a pen and pad. She'd written down that Roisin was to ring her sisters and tell them to put the kettle on in twenty minutes for their ETA of five forty-five pm.

Now she shoved Pooh's lead at Roisin before sitting on the sofa and opening her handbag for the pen and paper to begin scribbling.

'Mammy's after losing her voice, Bronagh,' Roisin explained.

Maureen's face was as mournful as a basset hound.

'Sure, that's not good timing with the reunion tomorrow, Maureen,' Bronagh clucked sympathetically.

'Aren't you supposed to be the entertainment?' Freya asked, frowning.

'I've got this, Mo,' Donal said, stepping in to save her from the writer's cramp. 'We're both supposed to be singing, Freya, but I'll have to fly solo if Mo's not up to it. It's a shame, but sure what can you do? And Roisin's Shay is bringing his fiddle, so it won't be a washout.'

Maureen held up the pad like a judge in an ice skating competition.

'I can still shake the tambourine,' Roisin read aloud.

Noah seized the moment and slid open Bronagh's drawer for biscuit seconds while the adults were otherwise engaged.

There was a murmur of agreement that all was not lost so long as she could shake her tambourine when footsteps sounded on the final flight of stairs leading down to the reception area. A creased-looking couple who, at a guess, Roisin decided would be in their middling fifties appeared. They had a shell-shocked aura as they surveyed the small huddle in the reception.

'Hello there, Mr and Mrs Richards,' Bronagh greeted the guests with a cheery smile, picking up her bag ready for the off. 'Did you catch up on a few hours of sleep then?'

'Please call us Cath and Ian.' Mrs Richards smiled as her husband placed their room key on the top of the reception desk. Freya took it and hung it alongside the other keys. 'And yes, we did, thanks.' The woman's gaze flicked to the sofa where Maureen was sitting, with Donal standing beside it, Roisin over by the brochures, and Pooh sat squarely in the middle. 'It's jet lag,' she explained, mustering a weary laugh as she added, 'we're not in the habit of afternoon siestas.'

Maureen put pen to paper and held up her pad. 'You're Australian?'

Unphased by the written enquiry, she said, 'Yes. Ian and I flew direct from Sydney to London, then on to Dublin. Our body clocks have no idea what the heck's going on.'

'It's a long way.' Maureen next held up.

'My mammy's after losing her voice,' Roisin explained.

'I see. That wouldn't be much fun.' Cath flashed Maureen a sympathetic smile.

'What brings you to Dublin's fair city then?' Donal asked.

Ian spoke up. 'I'm here for an architect's conference. Cath and I thought we'd make a holiday of it, given we've never visited Ireland before.'

'That sounds like a grand plan. I'm Freya, O'Mara's night receptionist and assistant manager, so if there's anything you need, please don't hesitate to ask.' Freya smiled.

'Well, you could start with a recommendation for dinner,' Cath said.

'Ah well, now that's easy. I've the perfect place for you, and it's only a short walk down the road. Quinn's Bistro. You won't find tastier traditional Irish fare and music anywhere.'

Aisling had coached Freya well, Roisin thought, although what she said was true enough. Her stomach rumbled at the memory of many a delicious meal enjoyed at her brother-in-law's restaurant.

The Australian announced that sounded just the ticket, and as Freya gave them directions, Maureen got busy again. Once she'd finished writing down her message, there was a tearing sound as she ripped the paper from the pad and held her note out to Donal. He scanned the text and gave Maureen a nod.

While Freya explained the couple was to turn right onto Baggot Street, Bronagh took the opportunity to say her goodbyes and sidled out the door. Donal jumped in as per his instructions as soon as Freya finished speaking.

'Maureen here was the proprietor of O'Mara's along with her late husband, Brian,' he said as Maureen nodded.

'Really?' Cathy turned her attention to the little woman with no voice ensconced on the sofa. 'It's a beautiful guesthouse.'

Ian agreed as he admired the tasteful décor sympathetic to the era of the house.

Maureen dipped her head once more and got busy with her pen as Donal elaborated. He explained Maureen and Brian had raised their four children in the apartment on the top floor. 'O'Mara's is still in the family because their second eldest daughter, Aisling, manages it these days.' Then, he introduced them all.

Noah treated the Australians to the sight of a crunched-up custard cream biscuit as he said hello and received a frown from his mother.

AN O'MARA'S REUNION

Seeing Freya flicking through a reservations file, Donal added, 'And since Aisling had twins a month ago, Freya here has been a marvel.'

Freya flashed an appreciative smile at Donal while Maureen held her notepad like a flashcard.

I decorated the guesthouse myself.

'Well, you did a stunning job,' Ian complimented.

Maureen beamed.

'He's a fan of neo-classical style,' Cathy explained.

As a one-sided conversation about Dublin's fine Georgian architecture ensued, Roisin excused herself and herded herself and Pooh up the stairs. She was desperate to tell her sisters that all their dreams had come true.

Mammy had officially lost her voice.

Chapter Six

'Where's Uncle Tom and Uncle Quinn?' Noah demanded once Aunty Moira had let him go. He scanned the living room area of the family apartment on the top floor of O'Mara's.

Roisin waved at Aisling, who was glued to the sofa with a cushion wrapped around her middle, where two babies lay, serenely attached to a bosom each. The beatific expression on Aisling's face made Roisin hanker for the baby days of old.

As for Noah, the sight of his Aunty Aisling and baby cousins saw him zone in for a closer look. Roisin fancied he'd be very good at biology by the time he reached high school. He certainly had a keen interest in the human anatomy.

He watched the proceedings for half a second, then, pointing to his aunty's boobs, commented, 'It's just as well you've got two of them.'

'It is Noah,' Aisling replied with a poker face.

'Hello there, Kiera, you get bigger and more beautiful each time I see you.' Roisin crossed the room to the playpen and plucked her niece from it. She was getting heavy, she thought, cuddling her. 'Who's a beautiful girl then?'

'She can't talk, Mummy. She's a baby,' Noah said in that know-it-all tone that reminded Roisin of Colin.

'Actually, you'd be wrong there, Noah,' Moira corrected. 'She's very chatty these days. She can say Mama, Dada, Papa and Nana. And she's very, very good at saying no.'

'No!' Kiera shouted, making them laugh.

'Who's a clever girl?' Roisin jiggled Kiera. She put the little girl down as she began to wriggle, wanting to roam the room now she was free from her playpen.

Noah was unimpressed and went back to watching the twins and his aunty.

Aisling remembering Noah's question of a minute ago, said, 'Your Uncle Quinn's at the restaurant, Noah. He had to ensure everything will run smoothly while we're away this weekend.'

'And Uncle Tom will be back any minute. He's out running.' Moira sighed. 'Again.'

'Still determinedly training for the Dublin Marathon, then?' Roisin moved toward Aisling for a peek at her niece and nephew. She was only half listening to Moira's reply that Quinn and Tom were still planning on entering the ridiculous long race. They were taking their training very seriously, she said.

'Pair of eejits that they are,' Moira muttered.

Kiera toddled over to say hello to Pooh, who'd gone straight to the doggy bed in the corner of the room. His head was resting on his paws, but seeing the advancing baby girl, it popped up in alarm.

Roisin squeezed onto the sofa next to Aisling, reaching over to stroke the twins' downy heads. 'I think they're going to have your colouring, Ash,' she said, fancying she could see reddish-gold glints in the soft peach fuzz catching the light overhead. She wished they'd hurry up and finish their feeds because she was desperate for a hold.

Moira scooped Kiera up before she could give Pooh a welcoming pull on his ear and suggested Noah be a magician.

The little boy was seemingly mesmerised by the twins having dinner, and Roisin was grateful for Moira's intervention. Her sixth sense was saying he'd bring up his school visit to the farm's milking sheds any second now.

His aunt's words caught his attention. 'A magician came to our school, Aunty Moira. He pulled a rabbit from his black hat.'

'Did he now? That was very clever of him.'

'No.' Noah frowned. 'It wasn't clever. It was magic.'

'Well, Kiera will think you're a magician if you hide this peg.' Moira produced a dolly peg from the pocket of her jeans and handed it to him. She sat Kiera down and retrieved a stack of plastic cups. 'Under these.' She set them out in a row, and Kiera began screeching like a parakeet. 'You see? She's excited because it's her favourite game.'

'It's not a very exciting game, Aunty Moira.' Noah inspected the wooden peg. 'I think it would be much better if I had a rabbit and a black hat. Or I could use Demi.'

There was a scrabbling in the gerbil cage housed on the sideboard.

'Could we not make do with the cups and peg?' Moira asked.

Roisin didn't need to drag her gaze from her beautiful niece and nephew to know Noah would have pursed his lips in a sure sign he wasn't convinced. If he was going to do something, he liked to do it properly. She doubted a peg and cups would cut the mustard for performing magic tricks.

Thirty seconds later, however, with one of his Aunty Aisling's snowballs in his gob, Roisin was proved wrong. She watched in amazement as he discovered his inner Penn and Teller with his limited stage props.

Roisin soaked up the convivial ambience of chilled-out sisters, content babies and a happy child. She thought, this was what it was all about, watching Noah lift the pink cup to reveal the peg with a 'Ta-dah!' Family togetherness.

Five minutes later, Maureen, Donal and a sweaty Tom appeared in the living room. They were greeted with barking, screaming and the sight of Moira and Roisin trying to pacify a poodle, a child and a toddler. Moira thrust Kiera at Tom. The sight of her dripping father only made her scream all the more.

'Jesus, Mary and Joseph! What's going on?' Maureen mouthed.

Roisin lipread her query and informed them what had happened over the din.

'Pooh snatched the dolly peg, ran over to his doggy bed, and sat on it. Noah can't do the magic show without it.'

The newcomers' eyes flicked to where Pooh was sprawled on his doggy bed with a butter wouldn't melt in his mouth look on his poodley face. As Moira tried to roll him off the bed to get at the peg, he bared his sharp little teeth at her.

'Pooh! Don't be such a bold boy,' Maureen mouthed ineffectually. She tried stamping her foot and clapping her hands to no avail, then tugged at Donal's sleeve and mouthed, 'Do something.'

Donal shrugged. 'He won't listen to me, Mo, you know that.'

'Why's Mammy after playing charades? Can't she see we've Armageddon going on?' Aisling asked, gently rubbing Aoife's back as she watched Maureen miming holding a microphone and singing at Donal.

No one answered as Maureen looked past Donal to her middle daughter on the sofa and jerked her thumb backwards in a 'get your arse up here now' way.

'Don't look at me, Mammy. I've the babies.' Aisling had been about to ask Roisin to wind Kieran when the furore over the dolly peg had erupted. Aoife gave a satisfying windy pop.

'Your mammy's lost her voice, Aisling,' Donal explained. 'I think she wants you to stand in for Dolly so we can duet the "Islands in the Stream" song because you know it works a treat on Kiera.'

Maureen nodded furiously.

'She's lost her voice?' Aisling looked to Roisin for confirmation, who'd been telling her son to stop carrying on like so.

Roisin nodded.

Sitting back on her haunches over by the doggy bed, Moira stared at her mammy.

'There'll be time for celebrations later,' Roisin said, the comment whizzing over the top of Maureen's head. 'Ash, Mammy's right. You've got the best voice out of a bad bunch.'

'Excuse me, I do an excellent Madonna under the right conditions,' Moira was indignant.

'Like a soundproof room,' Tom mumbled. Then added as Kiera gave a particularly ear-splitting wail, 'Let Aisling be Dolly.'

Roisin left Noah, determined not to be outdone by his cousin rolling around on the ground, and moved to take Kieran from her sister. 'I'll see to the wee man here. C'mon, Ash, you're our only hope.'

Roisin draped a muslin square from the pile on the coffee table over her shoulder and then carefully held Kieran.

Aisling sorted Aoife out and got to her feet. She stood next to Donal.

'Give it your all, Aisling,' Donal said, giving her the nod.

Maureen began to clap the intro, tapping her foot to an imaginary beat.

Kiera was equally sweaty from the screaming as her father from his running. She paused as her attention was caught by her beloved Poppa D beginning to sing. Meanwhile, Moira sped to the kitchen, returning with Aisling's bag of snowballs. She thrust the chocolate treats at Noah, rendering him silent, and was in time to watch Aisling close her eyes and channel her inner Dolly as she joined in the famous song.

She had the boobs for it, Roisin thought, wincing as her sister tried and failed to hit the high notes. Kiera didn't mind, though; her sobs slowed to sporadic hiccups.

Noah had contentedly begun chomping his way through the snowballs, and Pooh had rolled over for a tummy rub, revealing the cause of all the trouble in the first place.

The dolly peg.

Chapter Seven

The love on Tom's face as he held his arms out for his daughter made Roisin's chest ache. She watched as he confidently reached down and took Kiera from Maureen, holding her with practised ease. Her sisters had chosen well because both her brothers-in-law were hands-on fathers. It hadn't escaped her notice that it had been Tom who'd helped Kiera with her dinner and bathed her, not once checking in with Moira whether he was getting it right. Colin had left the practical side of Noah's babyhood to Roisin. That didn't mean he was a lousy father, but he'd seen his role as the provider more than the nurturer, and while he'd made a mess of that, she didn't doubt for a moment her ex-husband loved their son.

The news he was moving to Dubai was still sinking in, but she knew he firmly believed it would benefit their son in the long run. Colin had never understood that the most important thing you could give your child was time.

Her sigh was heavy as she eyed Noah with his chocolate-smeared face amusing himself by drawing on the piece of paper his nana had ripped off her pad for him. Resentment toward Colin and this failure of his to see the bigger picture swelled. He wouldn't be around to deal with the fallout as Noah tried to make sense of his father, whom he'd always seen regularly, suddenly becoming inaccessible. She blinked away the threatening tears. There'd be time for all that upon their return to London. For now, she focussed on her niece as Tom presented her for a kiss goodnight.

Roisin's lips rested against the soft, warm cheek as she breathed in the mix of lavender baby wash, talcum and milk. Was there anything yummier in the whole world than a sleepy, plump baby? she thought, savouring the moment. Kiera was worn out due to her award-winning performance earlier in The Dog Ruined The Game. The bedtime bottle Nana had given her, and the naughty puppy story Roisin read to her had finished her off.

'They're asleep for at least the next two hours,' Aisling announced as she joined them to await Donal's return from the Chinese takeaway. 'I'm starving.' She snatched up the empty packet of Snowballs and gave it a hopeful shake. Noah didn't look up from his drawing.

'Donal just rang from the takeaway to say he's on his way back,' Moira said, finishing setting the table.

It was a miracle there was a dinner order for Donal to collect in the first place, given the great debate on how they could narrow it down to just five dishes. It was Mammy's fault, of course, Roisin thought, pointing the finger of blame. She was the one who'd insisted it would be a shameful waste to order too much food, given none of them would be around to eat the leftovers on the weekend. So she'd scribbled on the Magna Doodle board that five dishes were ample.

Aisling hadn't taken Mammy's dictum lying down. 'But I'm breastfeeding, Mammy. I need sustenance.'

'There's sustenance, and then there's being the little piggy who had roast beef,' Moira butted in. 'And you're not to eat all the cashew nuts in the chicken and cashew dish either. Mammy, can I have duck yuk sung? It's my favourite.'

'Since when?' Maureen doodled.

'Since I tried it with Tom one time.'

Roisin cringed inwardly, waiting for it. She was tempted to put her hands over her eyes and peek through them because Noah's mouth had formed an 'O'. His eyes were suddenly too big for his head, aghast at having heard his Aunty Moira's flagrant use of a rude word.

'You swore,' Noah breathed half in awe, half in glee and not without a smattering of fear as he flicked his gaze between his aunty and nana to see what would happen next.

Roisin, listening to her son, thought to herself, I could have written the fecking script. Unfortunately, he had a track record when it came to ducks.

'I didn't.' Moira frowned, slow on the uptake.

'Noah,' Roisin warned, knowing it was futile but feeling she should, 'you don't need to repeat—'

'You said you wanted duck fuk for your dinner!' Noah said, upping the volume.

'Thanks a million, Moira.' Roisin pulled a face at her sister. 'Could you not just have ordered lemon chicken?'

'I said "yuk", Noah. Duck yuk with a "y".'

'Mummy, I'm not eating duck, yuck!' Alarm flickered in her son's eye.

Roisin appeased him by adding wontons to the order and daring her sisters to argue with her.

'What's wrong with good old chop suey?' Maureen held up the Magna Doodle again.

Moira's so-called swearing and the Magna Doodle board brought back memories because the board had belonged to Moira once upon a time. It was kept in the toybox tucked away in the cupboard in Patrick's old room. It had been her bright idea to unearth it for Mammy's use, and Roisin recalled how she used to take great delight in writing words that would have seen her mouth washed out with soap had Mammy caught sight of them. She never got caught, though, because when Aisling, claiming to be morally offended by her sister's doodling, returned with Mammy in tow, the board always had a clean slate.

Upon hearing the apartment door bang shut, there was a stampede for the table. Donal set down the bag holding the stack of containers, and they filled their plates and bellies. Even Pooh, for whom there was an emergency stash of dog biscuits on hand, was allowed a little bit of the beef and black bean sauce. The only upset in the meal was when Moira smacked her sister's hand with her spoon to make her drop the cashew nuts back into the chicken dish. However, everyone agreed it had been a tasty takeaway.

The clean-up was minimal, and Roisin expected Mammy and Donal to announce they'd get on their way. But, instead, Mammy retrieved the bag she'd left out in the hallway.

'Close your eyes,' she relayed via the Magna Doodle.

Aisling, Moira and Roisin sighed collectively, but Tom's eyes lit up.

'I like surprises,' he said obligingly, shutting his eyes.

'But if you can't speak, how will we know when to open them?' Roisin asked. It was a logical question to her mind, but she received the reply of 'Don't make me count to three, Roisin' on the Magna Doodle. So she closed her eyes, leaving her mammy to stare her sisters into submission.

There was an unzipping sound, and then a second or two later, Donal informed them they could open their eyes.

Maureen mouthed, 'Ta-dah!' and flapped the tee shirt she was holding like a matador enticing a bull.

'Ah, no, Mammy. You didn't,' Aisling groaned.

'Jaysus wept.' It was all Roisin could come up with.

'I'm not wearing that,' Moira informed her mammy.

Tom grinned. 'I think it's great. Although I'm not an O'Mara, so do I still get one?'

'Yer a fecky brown-noser Tom Daly,' Moira said.

'You, me, Quinn and Shay, we've all got one.' Donal grinned broadly. 'Maureen didn't want us to feel left out.' He draped a beefy arm across her shoulder and gave it a squeeze. 'And there's a spare one going for anyone who might want one.'

'Is there one for me, Nana?' Noah asked.

At least it would get him out of his Mickey Mouse shirt, Roisin thought, seeing her mammy nod before writing something.

'There's one for each of the babbies too.' Maureen's smile was wider than the Magna Doodle board she was displaying.

'No, Mammy. No child of mine will be wearing one of those. Sure there'll be photographs being taken.'

Maureen put the plain white tee shirt with the words "O'Mara Reunion 2002" down on the table and wrote furiously on the Magna Doodle. Then held it up. 'You'll wear it. And you'll like it. And I'll hear no more about it.'

Roisin read the message they'd heard growing up, only more often than not, it had been you'll eat it, and you'll like it.

'You might as well have had O'Mara eejits screen-printed on them, Mammy,' Moira moaned. 'Because that's what we'll all look like.'

'Don't tempt me, Moira. It's not too late.' Flashed up before them.

Chapter Eight

♥

Suzie kept step with Glen as he pushed the trolley through the doors and exited Cork Airport's only terminal building. She was eager to get to their hotel because, having caught sight of her rumpled reflection in the glass doors, she knew she was in desperate need of three things: a nap, a shower and a change of clothes. She never slept on planes, and the overnight flight from Dubai to Dublin, where they'd picked up their connecting flight to Cork, was taking its toll. Yet, despite her flagging energy reserves, she was excited because, having grown up in Brocton, Massachusetts, she'd always felt a solid connection to the country her ancestors had left behind. Suzie imagined this visit would feel like coming home.

She could only imagine what it felt like for Glen.

They were met by a gentle summery afternoon which was a far cry from the glitz and glare of the fast-paced city they'd left behind, and she waited, watching with a fond smile as Glen paused to gulp in lungfuls of fresh air.

It was different, all right. This was Ireland's high summer, but there was a crispness in the air that was a world away from Dubai's curious mix of hot, dry and humid weather. The UAE city's climate was one she and Glen often lamented they didn't think they'd ever get used to, especially this time of year when they were eternally grateful for that marvellous invention of air con. This was more like home, not that Suzie didn't love their life in Dubai. It was just it had never been her intention to live there forever. She'd had a wonderful time these last few years, but as her mom always said, life was a series of phases, and she was ready to move into the next one. It was time. She was hoping this weekend would help Glen realise he was too.

Suzie indulged him for a few seconds longer. He was entitled to savour this moment. It was the first time he'd returned to Ireland since leaving for England with his dad as a young boy. She wondered what was running through his mind, eyeing the face she knew so well.

She'd been at a hotel bar with a tiki theme the first time she'd seen him and had thought him ruggedly handsome, her opinion hadn't changed. Mel, her new friend, had dragged her there under duress shortly after she arrived in Dubai to take up the hotel receptionist role she'd been offered. So there she'd been with her fake orange lei draped around her neck, emboldened by the cheap mai tai's she'd been guzzling, eyeing his Romanesque nose and strong jawline as he leaned on the bar waiting for the drinks he'd ordered for him and his friends.

Mel's verdict had been he was craggily good-looking. For whatever reason, that description had made Suzie think of John Wayne. With his dark colouring, Glen was nothing like the star of the old Western films, although she'd loved him in the classic, *The Quiet Man*. Unlike the actor's piercing blue eyes, Glen's were sometimes green, sometimes brown, but no matter what the colour, they were always kind, with a permanent twinkle dancing in them. They'd reeled her in from the start when, feeling her gaze on him, he'd turned his head in her direction.

Now, though, his expression was inscrutable. Was he excited at finding his feet back on Irish soil, or was he wary and regretting his decision to return? He'd let snippets of his childhood slip now and again, and she'd gleaned enough to know it had been far from idyllic.

A breeze blew up from nowhere, and wisps of fine blonde hair tickled her face. She'd determinedly snatched back her hair with its penchant for knots, knowing she had a severe case of bed hair and secured it with a bobble before disembarking the plane. Seven-plus hours of trying and failing to get comfortable would do that, and she gave Glen a gentle nudge. 'Come on, I need to get my head on a pillow for a couple of hours, and you need a shave.'

Her words snapped Glen out of his reverie. 'Need a shave, do I?' He took his hands from the luggage trolley and made a sudden grab for her, making her squeal and then laugh as he tried to rub his stubbly cheek against hers. A suit-clad man with a briefcase hurrying past shot them an amused glance.

'Get off!' Suzie wriggled free, grinning up at him and then, dangling the car keys she was holding, said, 'The Avis man said to turn left outside the terminal and then it's only a short walk over there.' Her nails flashed unnaturally pink as she pointed to the covered walkway at the end of which was the car park where they'd been told they'd find the hatchback they'd hired. Was the varnish she'd chosen garish? She usually opted for a clear gloss for less maintenance, but she'd gone all out for this trip. Her hair was freshly highlighted, and she was sporting a tan that hadn't been there a week ago. There was a new silk dress from a designer boutique in her favourite souk and matching shoes carefully tucked away in her suitcase too.

The thought of the dress with its vibrant cerise colour and matching shoes that had seemed so perfect when she'd bought them made her nip at her bottom lip. There was no point in angsting whether they'd look over the top in the small village they were heading to, though, because it was too late to buy something more sedate now. Besides, it wasn't her that would be the focus of attention. All eyes were bound to be on Glen. As he turned the trolley sharply to the left, the carry-on bag tossed on top of their two cases wobbled precariously, and she held out a steadying hand, leaving it there as they made their way to the car park.

The silver hatchback they'd hired wasn't hard to locate, and after faffing with wing mirrors and seat angles, they exited the airport and got on the road. Suzie had been happy for Glen to drive, although this meant she was the chief navigator and wasn't sure she was up to the job.

The weariness plaguing her earlier was replaced by excitement, watching the countryside unfurl as they drove along. The colours were so bright they almost hurt her eyes. It had been a long time since she'd seen greenery this lush and velvety, and the glimpses of thrashing Atlantic coastline were breathtaking.

Her concern over her ability to navigate proved warranted when Glen veered the car inland an hour later, and they bounced along a narrow lane in the middle of nowhere.

'I think we're officially lost,' Suzie declared, woefully staring down at the map on her lap.

Glen puttered to a stop. 'Here, pass that over. You're a woman of many talents, Suze, but map reading ain't one of them.'

He was right, and she was glad to oblige, knowing her inability to drag her eyes away from the landscape surrounding them had probably seen her miss a vital turn-off on the map.

As he flattened the map against the steering wheel, his finger tracing the route they'd travelled, Suzie clambered out of the car. She stretched her arms high over her head, hearing a satisfying click.

A droning in the distance saw her shade her eyes with her hand to track its source, and in the patchwork of stonewalled fields beyond the blackberry hedgerow, she spied a tractor at work. Then, a happy sigh slipped from her lips, seeing the thatch-roofed wattle-and-daub farmhouse cottage perched on a gentle rise overseeing the land. It was all just as she'd pictured it would be.

The driver's door opened, and Glen's footsteps crunched over loose stones toward her. He slipped an arm around her waist and stared out at the vista. 'I'd forgotten all this.'

'It's beautiful.'

He didn't reply, but she felt him nod as they stood in contented silence bar for the tractor and an inquisitive bumble bee. Then, spying a plump blackberry, Suzie broke free and plucked it from the bush, offering it to Glen.

He grinned. 'Finders keepers.'

She popped it in her mouth, enjoying the berry's ripe juiciness as her eyes searched out another.

'I remember going blackberrying in the summer with my cousins,' Glen said softly. 'There were three of them, Patrick, Roisin and Aisling, who travelled down from Dublin on the bus to stay with us in Killybun for a week in the summer holidays a couple of times. I hope they're at the reunion. I'd like to catch up with them all.' He paused, and Suzie didn't interrupt, wanting him to tell her more.

'Their parents ran a guesthouse, so they couldn't leave it often. I loved it when they came to stay because the house seemed to come alive. Mam gave us free rein to come and go as we pleased. We must have looked like a sight by the time we rolled in looking for our dinner, mouths ringed with purple and fingers sore from the thorns having done our best to strip the bushes.' There was a smile in his voice, and Suzie leaned into him, picturing the little boy and the cousins he was describing.

'Who was related to your dad, Maureen or Brian?' She held her breath to see if his expression would become guarded, but he smiled at his childhood memories.

'Brian's father was my grandfather's brother, so I don't know what that makes him to me technically, but I always referred to him as my uncle, and we had a lot to do with him and the rest of the family even though Killybun was a good few hours south of Dublin. So I was sad to hear Brian passed away a few years ago, not long after my dad. Maureen wrote to us a few times when Dad and I went to live in London, but Dad never wrote back, so far as I know. He cut all ties.'

It wasn't often Glen mentioned his memories of growing up here in a small town not all that far from Claredoncally, where they were headed now, and more often than not when he did, they were tinged with bitter sadness. But to hear him talk with a smile in his voice gave Suzie hope that this trip would work out well after all.

It had taken him a year to trust her enough to confide the hurt he'd felt when his mother left him as a boy for reasons he said he'd never understand. Lately, though, Suzie realised they were reasons he refused to understand. Glen had taken what his father told him as gospel, and wouldn't be swayed from believing that his mother hadn't wanted him.

The night he'd opened up about his childhood, they'd been sitting in the garden of a quiet hotel framed by palm trees. They were enjoying an aperitif watching the red orb in the sky slowly begin its evening descent. She'd sipped her gimlet as he'd told her how his world had crumbled when he'd arrived home from school as a nine-year-old to find his mam gone. There'd been a note to say she'd gone to look after her sister, who wasn't well in Canada, but he'd known instinctively she wasn't coming back. His father had withdrawn, refusing to have his wife's name mentioned in the house. Then not long after Glen's tenth birthday, he'd announced they were moving to London.

Glen had told her his father had come out of his shell when he met Jenny, a secretary at the firm he worked for. It had been a relief to see him smiling again and a burden off Glen's young shoulders to know his father was happy. Hugh O'Mara had presented Jenny with a wedding band, which she wore, knowing they couldn't be wed in the eyes of the law because he wasn't divorced. To the world around them, though, they were married, which was enough for them both. It was as if a line had been drawn in the sand where his mother was concerned when Jenny moved in with them. Glen came to love Jenny and eventually almost managed to convince himself his mother had never existed in the first place.

Suzie always felt so sad thinking of the confused little boy he'd been. She empathised with the hurt he carried and counted her blessings regarding her boisterous, sometimes annoying but always loving family.

'So, are we lost?' she asked, peering down the lane but unable to see past the bend. 'Do I need to jump up and down to catch the farmer's eye and ask for directions?' It was said tongue in cheek. She might not rate as a map reader, but Glen's refusal to stop and ask for directions was the stuff of legends.

His laugh in response was almost melodious. 'We don't want to give the old fella too much excitement. We took a left instead of a right at that intersection a few miles back.' He sized the width of the lane. 'I don't fancy my chances doing a three-point turn. I'll have to reverse us out.' He stepped over a pothole and got back in the car.

Suzie didn't say anything as she settled back in her seat, and Glen twisted to see back over his shoulder before beginning to back out slowly.

If anybody had told her six months ago she'd be taking an impromptu holiday to Ireland, she wouldn't have believed them. So nobody had been more surprised than her by Glen's sudden announcement that he'd like to attend an O'Mara family reunion being held in a small village near Cork in late July. When he'd asked her to come with him, she hadn't hesitated to say yes.

She was thirty-six years old, thirty-seven in September, and she wanted more than work and the lifestyle in the Emirates that, with its endless rounds of eating out and ex-pat parties, somehow never felt permanent. She'd always assumed she'd settle down and have a family one day but the man she wanted to do that with had taken forever to come along. But now, he had, and she was ready to start that family. Glen, however, was damaged goods. The idea of marriage and bringing a child into the world terrified him, and she knew he had to make peace with his past to move forward. She hoped coming home to Ireland and facing his demons would do that.

Hugh had passed last year, and Jenny, unable to remain in the house in leafy Twickenham after his death, had gone to stay with her sister in Devon. Glen had volunteered to sort the house for sale after the funeral, and Suzie had remained in London to help him.

This was how she knew there were two sides to every story, because when Glen refused to read through the letters she'd found from his mother, unopened in a shoe box at the bottom of his father's wardrobe, she'd kept hold of them even though he'd told her to bin them. She didn't plan to open them. They weren't hers to read, she told herself each time she unearthed them from where she'd tucked them at the bottom of her underwear drawer to stare at the flowing handwritten address. The unanswered question at the forefront of her mind would burn. Why? Why had she left? And in the end, like Eve with the apple, temptation had proved too much.

Glen was away in Germany on business and, alone in their apartment, she'd retrieved the bundle, sifting through them until she found one dated the year his mother had left her family. Her hand had trembled as she slipped it open, and there was a moment's hesitation as to whether she should stop now before it was too late and bin the lot like Glen had told her to. But she hadn't, choosing instead to read it and the next one and the next, not stopping until the last.

Dara O'Mara, or Hickey as she'd reverted to, hadn't vanished from her son's life. On the contrary, she'd tried her hardest to stay in contact with him, but Hugh, for reasons he felt strongly enough about, had refused to allow it.

Oh yes, there were two sides to every story.

Suzie knew she was playing with fire when she wrote to Dara at the address on the back of the last letter she'd sent, asking her to reply to her work address at the hotel. She'd explained Glen knew nothing about her writing to her and posted it before she could change her mind. The weeks passed, and Suzie convinced herself the woman would have long since moved. If by some miracle, Dara did get her letter, too much water had passed under the bridge. She wouldn't reach out now.

But she did write back.

The truth wasn't always black and white. Sometimes it was murky shades of grey, and when Suzie read Dara's letter, it was clear what she had to do.

As for Ireland, Glen had chosen to stay away all these years. His memories of his mother and childhood were tangled up in this place. Now, she observed the concentration on the face of the complicated Irishman she loved with all her heart.

They were heading for make-or-break time, and this trip would seal the deal either way.

Chapter Nine

Roisin couldn't hear what she was saying as her voice was overridden by the farting sound the clapped-out old banger was making. Tom had put his foot down, determined to accelerate up to the speed limit. However, the gist of what Moira was trying to get across was clear as she jabbed at the bullet points. They listed their ETA at various points along their journey to Claredoncally. On the flip side of the paper was the lowdown of what to expect throughout the weekend.

It had been a slow crawl out of Dublin with Aisling, Quinn, the twins and Freya leading the way. Aisling called their new family wagon the tank, and she wasn't far wrong, Roisin mused, seeing it up ahead. She wondered how Freya was getting on in the back seat there with the twins.

The Friday traffic was heavy, but they'd finally reached the motorway and were southbound. Tom was swearing at the car's reluctance to pick up speed. Moira's teeth were gritted as though they might take off at any second, like Chitty Chitty Bang Bang. Meanwhile, Roisin looked over her shoulder to see if Mammy, Donal and Noah were still bringing up the rear. She couldn't see them, however, for the cloud of black smoke trailing behind Moira and Tom's car.

Moira moaned, 'And I can't believe we have to wear these stupid shirts, can you?'

This time, Roisin caught what she was saying as Tom saw the speedometer reach the limit and eased off the gas.

'Look on the bright side, Moira. At least we won't see anyone we know in Claredonwotsit.'

'Roisin, of course we will. It's a fecking family reunion.'

'Family doesn't count because they're O'Maras, so they're bound to look eejity themselves.'

'Good point, and it's just as well it's being held in culchieville and not Dublin' – Moira sniffed – 'or my street cred as an edgy art student would be shot.'

Roisin wasn't sure if Moira was serious or not.

'Did you cop a load of Aisling in hers? Jaysus wept. The sight of her chest straining to get out of that tee shirt hurt my eyes, so it did.' Moira shook her head. 'Quinn's eyes popped out of his head when she came out in it this morning. It's just as well the twins and Freya are in the car with them, or they'd be pulling off down the first quiet country lane for the riding. Poor Tom here didn't know where to put himself, and I thought Donal would expire with the coughing fit he was after having. And look at the state of this.' Moira tugged at her oversized shirt. 'I could have worn this when I hit the ninth-month mark carrying Kiera.'

Roisin laughed. 'Mine is just as bad. We look like we should be backup singers from an 80s Wham video wearing Choose Life shirts.'

'What are you on about?'

'Before your time, Moira.'

'Maureen didn't do great on the sizing,' Tom spoke up. 'I feel like I'm going to burst out of mine.'

'I quite like that look on you.' Moira eyed him up as though she'd spied a tasty piece of meat in the local butcher's window. 'It's very James Dean, only instead of "Rebel Without a Cause", you've "O'Mara Reunion 2002" written across your chest.' She sniggered.

Tom cut her a look.

'So you've heard of James Dean and *Rebel Without a Cause*, but you don't know about Wham and the Choose Life shirts? That's just wrong, Moira.' Roisin began to snap her fingers and hum "Wake Me Up Before You Go-Go" but stopped as Kiera's bottom lip trembled.

'I've only heard of it because Patrick had a James Dean poster in his bedroom.'

Roisin snorted, and Kiera's eyes widened in alarm. 'Jaysus wept! I'd forgotten about that. You want to have seen the state of him, Tom. It was before he discovered Billy Idol and the rebel yell. He was always very impressionable, Patrick. He saw the movie one Saturday afternoon on the television, and the next thing he's getting about the place thinking *he's* a rebel without a cause. I caught him practising his broody James Dean in the bathroom mirror. Instead of a cigarette in his hand, he'd pinched a Tampax from the box in the drawer.'

'It was a foregone conclusion he'd wind up with a woman who is the face of personal care products then.' Moira snickered.

Roisin laughed, then, seeing Kiera begin to squirm, began crooning the "Wheels on the Bus". She made the rolling wheel motions with her hands.

Kiera began to buck against the car seat restraints, clearly not a fan of what had been one of Noah's top-five car sing-songs as she shouted, 'No!'

Moira angled around, catching sight of her daughter's distress. 'Rosi, I told you. It's only the country music songs she likes. It's Mammy's fault. She's brainwashed her. I think she was a Moonie leader in another life. Try "Jolene" or maybe a bit of Shania. Failing that, Tom and I will do the "Islands in the Stream" song. Where's Foxy Loxy? He might settle her, or you could give her the flip-flop.'

Roisin spotted Kiera's favourite cuddly toy abandoned on the car floor. She reached down for it and snuged the soft fox toy Tom had given to Moira before Kiera was born alongside her. Poor Foxy Loxy was scowled at, and Roisin sighed, beginning a search and rescue mission for the flip-flop. Unfortunately, this had somehow made its way halfway under the driver's seat and she couldn't reach it. A big sigh escaped because she didn't want to have to do this, but it looked like she had no choice, so she began humming the opening bars of Dolly's "Jolene".

Kiera's reaction made her feel like a snake charmer playing his instrument. The baby girl's gaze fixed on her Aunty Rosi, and she swayed her head back and forth as her aunt sang about the other woman with eyes of green and auburn hair. She did her best and improvised the odd line but Kiera didn't care. By the fifth round Roisin was beginning to sound like Mammy had earlier.

'Aunty Rosi's got to rest her voice, Kiera.'

Kiera blinked at her aunty. 'No.'

Roisin held her breath, hoping she'd not be forced to sing it again but the steam had gone out of the little girl. It was a relief when she rested her head on Foxy Loxy and her eyes fluttered shut.

'She should have left him.' Moira sniffed.

'Who?' Roisin asked.

'Yer woman singing about Jolene.'

'Dolly?' Tom interjected.

'No, you eejit, Dolly sang the song about the woman whose husband was carrying on with yer Jolene wan.'

Roisin let her mind drift as Tom and Moira debated the point. What would Shay make of his shirt? she thought. She was glad Mammy had included him on the O'Mara's Reunion tee-shirt front. And despite her gripes about this weekend it would be nice for him to spend more time with her sisters and their other halves. Mammy and Donal would have the chance to get to know him better too.

What would the hotel be like? Mammy had booked it. Apparently, it was the only hotel in the village so she'd not been spoiled for choice. Still, Great Aunt Noreen had assured mammy it was perfectly adequate. Noah had asked if he could sleep in the same room as his Nana and Poppa D which had been fine by Roisin.

Anticipation at the thought of her and Shay having the room all to themselves whipped through her, but before she could begin daydreaming a strong smell brought her to her senses.

'Tom was that you?' Moira was demanding.

'It was not.'

'Rosi? Because I can tell youse both it wasn't me.'

'No!' Roisin leaned toward Kiera and sniffed. 'It's your daughter, thank you very much.'

'We'll have to pull over for a nappy-change pit stop,' Tom said, beginning to indicate for the upcoming Kildare exit.

'But it's not on the itinerary.' Moira flapped the sheet of paper that stated they would be calling in for a triple nappy change and cup of tea in Portlaoise. 'You know what Mammy's like. She'll go mad.'

'It's not mammy whose after sitting in the back with that smell now, is it? Take the exit, Tom,' Roisin said.

Tom mouthed 'sorry' at his wife and veered off the motorway.

As it happened Maureen and Donal had been listening to Noah chanting he needed a wee since before they'd exited the big smoke. This was despite Maureen checking to ensure he went before they set off.

It had taken several circuits of the town centre to find parking to accommodate them, with Quinn apparently refusing to pay for parking as he bypassed the pay and display facilities. This was not something they'd known about Quinn. Moira and Roisin agreed as Tom, with his head hanging out the car window gulping at the fresh air, muttered expletives about his marathon running partner.

At last they slotted in to various short-term spots, and any discord over Quinn's refusal to pay for parking was forgotten. This was because they were too sidetracked by his ability to parallel park the tank.

The family congregated on the pavement once pushchairs had been unloaded. It was agreed with the bonhomie of being on holiday that it was good to be flexible when you had babbies and a small child in tow. Sure what did it matter if they had their morning tea here instead of Portlaoise? Aisling had piped up.

Maureen wrote a note to say she'd be asking them to hand their respective itineraries in so she could cross out Portlaoise and replace it with Kildare. Then she accosted a local with her Magna Doodle board to enquire where the public toilets were. They were helpfully directed to Market Square and set off in single file down the busy narrow pavements of the ancient market town.

'Don't be touching anything, girls. Hover over the seat. And that includes you, Freya, because I'll not have you picking up the germs on my watch.' Maureen scribbled in shorthand before following her daughters and Freya into the building.

Noah, who'd refused to go to the ladies toilets with his mother, had insisted Poppa D escort him. This left Tom and Quinn standing outside in their O'Mara Reunion 2002 muscle shirts.

'I feel like an eejit,' Quinn muttered, seeing a group of young girls pointing and sniggering in their direction.

'So do I,' Tom said. 'Do you think we'll have to wear them all fecking weekend?'

'Yeah, I do.'

'Feck.'

'Yeah.'

Chapter Ten

'Would you look at that.' Roisin with her nose pressed to the window stared in awe at the dramatic sight presiding over the countryside. There, on a limestone outcrop was an imposing castle. 'The Rock of Cashel,' she breathed.

Moira gave the historic site a cursory glance. She wasn't overly fussed on castles and the like and had often been heard proclaiming that if you'd seen one of the old stone yokes you'd seen them all. True to form she said, 'Mammy's allowed us half an hour to explore the castle after lunch. I hope she's paying the entrance fee because I don't know how whoever runs these old places can sleep at night with what they charge you to go and poke around. Sure it's only a pile of old stone. It's a national disgrace so it is.'

'Actually, it's not a castle,' Tom said craning his neck for a look himself. 'It's the traditional seat of the Kings of Munster but one of them donated it to the church so the building you can see up there is a cathedral.'

Moira and Roisin stared at Tom, who shrugged.

'We visited it years ago on a family holiday. Something must have sunk in after all because I remember being bored silly by what I saw as a pile of mouldy old stones.'

Moira squeezed his leg. 'I knew you were my soulmate.'

Tom grinned at her in a way that made Roisin clear her throat as a reminder she was sitting in the back seat lest he get any ideas, and was pleased to see his gaze return to the road ahead.

'All I was bothered about was whether Dad would buy us an ice cream in the town afterward.' He laughed at the memory. 'I don't know how we all fit in the car, but somehow Mam and Dad crammed us kids in. We used to play I spy. Anybody up for a game?'

'No.' Moira was straight to the point.

'There were no seatbelts in the back, that's how. They were very lax about children's safety in the early eighties,' Roisin said. 'It's a miracle any of us made it to adulthood. And I'll second Moira on the game. It doesn't hold happy memories for me because the only family road trip we ever went on was when Mammy and Daddy took us around the Ring of Kerry. All I spied while we played I spy was Moira's sick all over me.'

'It wasn't my fault I got carsick.' Moira was on the defence. 'Mammy should have let me sit up the front and I'd have been grand. Sure look it, have I complained about feeling sick once today?'

'Fair play,' Roisin said to her sister with a grin. 'I don't suppose I can call you Moira Vomit Head anymore.'

'You were mean to me, so you were, you and Aisling.'

'Can you blame us like? She was a proper tell-tale, Tom, and being the baby of the family, she got away with murder.'

'Still does,' Tom replied.

'I heard that.'

Roisin and Tom laughed while Kiera made a sweet, snuffling sleepy sound.

Once they'd done the obligatory circuits seeking free parking, the town of Cashel was a quaint surprise.

'I'm starving,' Aisling announced to no one in particular as they assembled.

'Who's for a pub lunch, then?' Quinn rubbed his hands together.

Maureen's scribbling rendered them silent while they waited for her answer. She wielded the Magna Doodle at her son-in-law. 'I don't think so Quinn.'

'Why not?' Quinn was feeling bold.

An eyebrow shot up upon hearing this boldness and Maureen busied herself writing again.

Quinn read aloud, 'Look at the itinerary.' He turned to his wife. 'Pass me it please, Aisling.' Quinn waited while his wife, boobs a bouncing, hurried back to the car where she fetched it from the rubbish bag. She attempted to smooth out the crumpled paper as she returned to the group.

Upon seeing the state of her carefully crafted programme, Maureen ave her daughter a look that suggested she was seriously considering writing her out of the will.

Quinn offered Maureen an apologetic glance as he took the itinerary from Aisling. At the same time, Moira muttered fecky and brown-noser under her breath. He scanned the type for the bullet point with Cashel next to it and saw a forty minute slot had been allocated for a picnic. On cue, Donal appeared with a picnic basket in one hand, thermos in the other. Noah was by his side with a folded rug resting on his outstretched arms. He looked in danger of toppling forward and Roisin took it from him.

Quinn made a mental bet it would be egg sandwiches and a flask of tea he'd be having for his lunch, not beer battered cod with a mound of chips and a pint.

He realised Maureen had been busy once more as she tapped the board to get his attention. This time he read: 'Do you think a pub will be able to have us all fed and watered in forty minutes?'

Quinn was about to say, 'we could let them try,' when he stopped, looking at the familiar faces all watching the exchange for a clue, nervous in case he gave the wrong answer.

Maureen scribbled the answer out for him. 'No.' Then turning on her boat shoes, she set off and if she'd had an umbrella she'd have held it sky high as she ordered them to follow her. How she knew where to find a sunny patch of grass for them to sit down on was one of life's mysteries, but find it she did.

Roisin flapped the rug out on the grass and the twins were deposited on to it. Their little legs kicked about and Kiera, plopped next to them, promptly stood up and attempted a getaway. Noah took it upon himself to police his cousin, dragging her back over to the mat. He told her to stay there, thank you very much, in a voice uncannily like his mother's when she told him off.

'I hope you all like egg sandwiches,' Donal announced cheerily, unpacking the contents of the picnic basket.

'I knew it,' Quinn muttered, receiving an elbow in the ribs from his wife who was partial to the egg sandwich.

'Ah no Mammy they make Tom fart, so they do,' Moira moaned.

'Moira!' Tom said. 'Some things are sacred between husband and wife. You don't need to share everything.'

The board flashed a beat or two later. 'Get them down youse! There's children in Africa starving don't you know.'

Aisling, experiencing panic that there wouldn't be enough to go around swooped. She needed to be sure she got her share because she was breastfeeding two babbies.

Roisin played mother, pouring tea into plastic cups and soon they were all eating and drinking. Quinn moved on from his pique at missing out on his pub grub when Maureen produced the millionaire's shortbread for afters along with an apple each.

Noah, attempting a second piece of the chocolate and caramel treat turned his nose up at the fruit but was told there'd be no seconds until he ate the apple.

'Apples make Tom fart, too,' Moira shared.

Freya turned red on Tom's behalf as she dutifully gnawed on her apple. She would have liked a second piece of the millionaire's shortbread also, but was too frightened of Maureen not to eat her fruit first.

Once she'd stuffed herself silly, Aisling nursed Aoife and Kieran. At the same time, Kiera had fun mashing her sandwich into her face, managing to get egg in her hair.

They finished lunch within the allotted time frame – to Maureen's delight – and were set to head back to their cars when Roisin's scream shattered the peaceful vibe. All eyes spun toward her.

Roisin, her face a mottled red, was standing with her hand to her mouth.

'What is it?' Maureen mouthed. She expected the histrionics from Moira, but Roisin was stoic with her yoga breathing, which implied she was afflicted by something terrible.

'Tell her to do the yoga breathing,' Maureen tried to convey, but nobody could understand her and there was no time for charades or the Magna Doodle board.

'I've been stung,' Roisin said in a thick and muffled voice as the initial shock subsided.

Tom donned his imaginary white doctor's coat and went to her aid. 'It's a bee sting on the side of her lip by the looks of it.'

'At least it didn't get the babbies.' Aisling cradled Aoife closer to her chest, as did Quinn with Kieran.

'Kiera would have tried to eat it,' Moira said.

There was a collective wincing as Tom gently flicked out the stinger.

'Have we white vinegar?' Aisling asked. 'That's what you always put on them when we hobbled back from the green with them as kids, Mammy.'

'Oh sure, Aisling, there's a bottle of white vinegar just rolling around in the boot waiting for occasions like this.'

Aisling scowled at Moira.

Maureen held up the Magna Doodle. 'No but I've the E45 cream in the first aid kit.'

'I don't think E45 cream will do the trick, Maureen. She could do with an icepack, because that's starting to swell up nastily,' Tom advised.

Roisin whimpered.

Maureen's lips tightened. She'd two very bold son-in-laws today.

'You shouldn't have said that about the E45 cream,' Moira said. 'It's a cure-all.'

'Mummy, you look like those yucky Bratz dolls we saw in the toyshop,' Noah observed.

'More like Goldie Hawn in that *The First Wives Club* film,' Aisling said.

'Also some ibuprofen will help or an antihistamine.' Tom finished his inspection of Roisin's rapidly swelling lip.

There was an exodus back to the car with heads turning at the sight of the woman with the enormous top lip. The word on the street was a celebrity was in their midst because everybody knew they were always fiddling with their faces. There was further proof in so much as she was flanked by an entourage. One or two tourists aimed their cameras at Roisin, eager for a snapshot of the mystery celeb on the loose in Cashel. The burly fellow who looked like Kenny Rogers shielded her from public glare.

Roisin, fed up with the attention, clambered into the car's back seat, slinking down low. Upon seeing the state of Moira and Tom's car, a murmur of disappointment rippled through the crowd and those who'd produced pen and paper for an autograph stuffed them back in their bags. Of course, no bona-fide celebrity would be caught dead in a rust mobile like that and they quickly dispersed. However, one woman paused seeing Moira to enquire whether she was your Demi Moore wan.

Donal fetched the first aid kit and as luck would have it there was no antihistamine or ibuprofen in it. So he volunteered to find a pharmacy and Maureen flashed him with the Magna Doodle to ask him to pick up more of the Fisherman Friends.

Roisin leaned forward in the gap between the driver and passenger seats to inspect her lip in the rear-view mirror and felt like crying. So much for the ridey weekend she'd planned for herself and Shay. He'd be lucky if he fit in the hotel room with her and her lips.

Chapter Eleven

♥

'I think Mammy's going to surprise us with a night in the Bantry House,' Moira said. 'I wonder if it's a four-poster bed we'll be after sleeping in tonight, Tom?'

Tom gave her an indulgent smile. 'With a fireplace in the room.'

'Definitely. And peacocks roaming the grounds.'

'You're dreaming, both of you,' Roisin mumbled through her puffy lips, thinking Mammy better not have decided to treat them all to a luxurious night's accommodation before heading through to Claredonwotsit in the morning because it would be wasted without Shay there with her to enjoy it.

'Well, why else didn't she write it on the itinerary?' Moira queried, scanning the paper once more in case she'd missed something in the small print. 'No. It's definitely not written on there.'

'I thought it said we were staying at a hotel in Claredoncally, tonight,' Tom said. 'And I overheard Donal checking with Freya as to whether it was alright with her if we arrived there a few hours later than originally planned. She was of course. I mean she could hardly say no, given it's a free ride she's been given with Aisling and Quinn.'

'Not exactly free, she's helping with the twins,' Roisin said.

'It might say Claredoncally on the itinerary, but Mammy can be sneaky when she wants and she could have just included that on it to throw us off the scent like.'

Roisin picked lint off her Mo-pants. Moira was like a dog with a bone when she got an idea in her head. 'It's not likely, and what about Freya? I can't see her stumping up for five star accommodation for Emer's daughter can you?'

Moira was quiet while she thought about this. She was reluctant to let her luxury accommodation surprise go. 'Maybe she's after doing a Christmas in July bonus. Aisling's always going on about how she doesn't know how she'd manage without Bronagh and Freya. And think about it, Roisin. Bantry is out of our way. What other reason could she have for whisking us off to see an old house by the sea? Because you know yourself, you've seen one mouldy pile of stones you've seen them all.'

'History wasn't her thing at school, Tom.'

'I'm picking up on that, Rosi.'

'And Mammy wouldn't treat Freya and not Bronagh. That wouldn't be fair. Besides, I thought you said Bantry House was a mouldy pile of old stones not luxury accommodation. You can't have it both ways,' Roisin said grumpily. 'Cop yourself on.'

'It's what's on the inside that counts,' Moira replied sanctimoniously.

'How's the lip, by the way?' Tom, sensing sisterly tension, changed the subject.

Roisin looked up to meet her brother-in-law's gaze in the rear-view mirror. 'Still enormous, as you can see, but not itchy since I took the antihistamine, thanks.'

Moira twisted her head back to see for herself. 'Jaysus wept. It's like looking at that camel I went for a ride on when I was on my holidays in Tunisia.'

'I didn't know you'd been to Tunisia,' Tom said.

Moira nodded. 'For a week, all-inclusive like with an ex-boyfriend called Gerry. It was a nightmare because he was blond and everywhere we went he turned heads. It was like being on holiday with Brad Pitt.'

'I remember that. Your nose was right out of joint when you got home because nobody paid you the slightest bit of attention all week.' Roisin chortled, feeling her lips vibrating. It was a peculiar sensation.

'I haven't heard of a Gerry before either. How many fellas have you been out with?' Tom raised an eyebrow in Moira's direction.

Roisin knew he wasn't the jealous type, but there was bemusement in his tone nonetheless and she seized her chance to jump in with, 'Loads, Tom, loads. She wasn't picky. Ask Mammy.'

'Feck off,' Moira said. 'Anyway the camel ride was terrifying. It was a horrible, big smelly thing that kept trying to bite the other camels. And it made this awful noise. It was a sorta bleat-groan.' She made a guttural sound from the back of her throat causing Kiera to stir. 'Like that it was.'

'Don't you dare wake her,' Roisin hissed. 'And I do not look like a camel.'

The drive to Bantry took just over an hour and the crunching of tyres on gravel saw Roisin, who'd been drifting off thanks to the antihistamine, jolt awake. She rubbed her eyes and then, realising she'd been drooling, swiped her chin. It took a moment for her to soak in her surrounds. Behind them was an expanse of sparkling water – Bantry

Bay – and they were pulling into a car-parking area empty save for a tour bus. There was a building nearby Roisin supposed must have been the stables back in the day. She was keen to stretch her legs and clambered out, seeing the rest of their small tour party doing the same. To be fair, she was curious herself as to why Mammy had suddenly announced they were off to visit this old house, grand as it may be, and from what she could see it was certainly that.

'Tom, I'll leave you to fetch Kiera. I want to get a head start on Roisin and Quinn so we get the best bedroom. Oh and don't bother getting the pushchair out. I wouldn't think there'd be lifts in the place. She'll want to stretch her wee legs and then she can go in the backpack.' Moira legged it over to where Mammy and Donal were trying to cajole Noah, who'd locked himself in the car, out.

Roisin followed behind her to see what was up with Noah.

'He said the place reminded him of the Addams Family house on the DVD he watched with his daddy,' Donal informed Roisin. 'And that he's frightened your Wednesday wan will try to fry him in electric chair like she did Pugsley.'

'I told Colin not to let him watch that film.' Roisin sighed.

'Shall we try the bribery? There's a tea rooms over there. They're bound to have crisps or cake,' Maureen wrote on her board.

'That should work, Mammy.'

'Noah.' Roisin tapped on the window. 'If you come and have a walk around with us we'll let you choose something from the tea rooms after.'

'What about Wednesday?'

'You don't need to be worrying about her. It's America she lives in not Bantry, Ireland.'

Noah weighed up what his mother had said and in the end the thought of crisps or cake did the trick and he unlocked his door and clambered out. 'Will you hold my hand when we go inside, Poppa D?'

Donal donned a serious face. 'I will, Noah. You'll be safe with me.'

'Now that's sorted, I've something I'd like to say,' Moira announced, then cleared her throat waiting for everyone's full attention.

Maureen clasped her hands together and forgetting to rest her voice in her excitement whispered, 'Another grandchild on the way? My cup runneth over. But it would overflow if the pair of you would trot down the aisle first.'

Tom appeared completely bewildered as he jiggled Kiera into place in the backpack he'd donned to transport her around.

'Mammy, we're a modern couple. We don't need to be married to cement our relationship or to be a good mammy and daddy.'

Aisling leaned in and whispered to Roisin, 'He hasn't asked her yet. She'd say yes in a heartbeat if the diamond was big enough.'

'And, we're not having another baby either. Although you never know your luck if it's the four-poster bed we're after getting.' She flicked her hair over her shoulder and gave a terrified looking Tom a come-hither glance.

'Stop frightening Tom there. You know he's in training for the marathon,' Aisling bossed.

Now it was Maureen who was completely bewildered as to what exactly was going on here.

'What I wanted to say was it's very generous of you and Donal, Mammy,' Moira announced.

Aisling and Quinn, busy strapping twins into front packs, paused and Aisling asked, 'Mammy, Donal what's she on about? Is the entrance fee very expensive?'

'You're not to be paying me in, Maureen,' Freya said.

'But it's investigative work for O'Mara's. If we enjoy ourselves we can recommend it to guests. Mammy will keep the receipts, won't you, Mammy?'

Freya didn't look convinced and Maureen was waiting for Moira to get on with her announcement even though she was deflated after getting her hopes up like so.

Roisin, who knew Emer's reputation when it came to sponging off Great Aunt Noreen was pleased to see Freya didn't take after her mother, who'd have been only too happy for someone else to foot the bill.

'Is that how you're playing it, Mammy? A business expense. Well I'm not usually one for the old buildings and the like but I've got a feeling the accommodation will be charming.' Moira fixed Aisling in her line of sight. 'Bags the four-poster bed.'

'We're not staying here are we?' Freya's eyes widened in alarm. She was happy to pay her own way but doubted she could stretch to a night here nor did she want her mam sulking over her late arrival for the duration of the reunion either.

Maureen was set to begin writing in earnest but Donal placed a hand over hers.

'Now, now slow down, everyone. Moira, I think you've the wrong end of the stick. And no, Freya, we're not staying. It's a visit we're after having. We're booked into the hotel in Claredoncally and you'll be off to see your mam and aunt tonight. It says so on the itinerary.'

Moira's face fell while Roisin shot her an 'I told you so' look and Freya exhaled in relief. Meanwhile, Quinn, Tom and Aisling hadn't a clue as to how Moira had put two and two together and made five.

'And the reason we decided to make this side trip to Bantry House was because Maureen's after telling me on the Magna Doodle that your late Daddy wanted to visit it but he never got here. I suggested we call in as a sort a pilgrimage if you like.'

'But we did the road trip around the Ring of Kerry and it's not all that far from here, so why didn't we call in?' Moira asked.

Roisin flashed back to being cramped in the back of the family's old beemer with Moira complaining about feeling sick for the second time that day. Daddy driving had been over Mammy doing the pretend braking in the passenger seat because he was keen to jam as many sights into the family road trip as he could. That's when Moira had thrown up all over Roisin and it had been decided that it was for the best they head for home after that. She brought Moira up to date.

'It wasn't my fault.' Moira looked to Mammy then Aisling and finally Roisin. 'I should have been allowed to sit in the front seat.' She repeated her earlier comment to her sister.

'Fair play. It's ancient history,' Aisling said.

'You wouldn't say that if it had been you she was sick over.'

'Rosi, move on. The fact of the matter is our daddy never got to see Bantry House,' Aisling replied.

Roisin's eyes misted. 'You're right. And I think that's a perfectly grand reason to visit, Mammy. And thank you, Donal, for suggesting it.' She linked her arm through her mammy's and they set off to find the reception area.

Chapter Twelve

♥

It took them one and a half circuits of the enormous redbrick block house surrounded by carefully clipped gardens to locate the area where they could purchase their tickets. As it happened, it was tucked away near the tea rooms and once they'd paid their entry it was decided to have a wander around the gardens first to enjoy some fresh air and a stretch of the legs. They'd explore the house after. Noah had been quick to interject, that he thought it best the visit to the tea rooms for his cake or crisps was to come before visiting the house as he trudged alongside his Poppa D into the gardens.

'How many chimneys do you think the house has, Poppa D?'

'Too many to count, Noah.'

Roisin smiled listening to him tell Noah how there'd have been loads of servants back in the day to keep all the fires burning in all the rooms. She paused as they reached the fountain contained within a wisteria circle to read from the brochure she'd helped herself to. 'There's seven terraces and at the bottom of the gardens are one hundred steps leading to the woodland. Do you think you could run up those, Noah?'

Noah looked at his mammy. 'I think I could but only if I was allowed a drink with my crisps or cake.'

She smiled. 'I think we could stretch to a drink, too.'

'Mummy are you trying to smile?' Noah fixated on his mother's mouth. 'Because you look like Batman's enemy in that film Daddy let me watch.'

Fecking Colin, Roisin silently cursed her husband and his DVD choices. So far, she'd been likened to a Bratz doll, a camel and now the Joker. Meanwhile Moira, in close vicinity, was sniggering at Noah's pass remarking. Her jovial mood had been restored by Mammy paying her entrance into the house and gardens.

The small group meandered the grounds, enjoying the fresh air and balmy weather as they admired the artistry of the Italian garden. It was so well manicured, Quinn had been heard to remark that it made you wonder if they trimmed the bushes with scissors. Maureen true to form insisted on a group photograph being taken alongside the Diana the Huntress statue, which Freya offered to take given she wasn't immediate family. Maureen wouldn't hear of it though, pulling in O'Mara's night receptionist to stand next to Aisling. A couple strolling past with a picnic basket were roped in to taking the picture. Roisin hoped there was nothing hot to eat in their basket because it would have been cold by the time Mammy had finished arranging them like so. They'd all agreed as the couple legged it with their basket once they'd handed the camera back to Maureen, they'd been very patient.

There were plenty more photo opportunities given the gorgeous vista the house provided with Bantry Bay, Whiddy Island and the Cahal mountains for a backdrop. What would it be like to open your curtains of a morning to such a view, Freya had said to nobody in particular. By the time they were satisfied they'd snapped enough pictures to be assured they'd each have at least one for their respective albums where their heads weren't lopped off, Noah had returned to

AN O'MARA'S REUNION

the fold. He was red-faced and hot after his run up and down the stairs to the woods on the periphery of the gardens.

'Mum, I'm thirsty,' he panted.

They all fancied a cold drink and ventured into the tea room to enjoy a break before embarking on their tour of the house. It took forever to order given Maureen insisted on giving the young woman behind the counter, who'd made the mistake of showing interest in their matching tee shirts, the run down on the O'Mara family reunion via the Magna Doodle.

'Brian would have enjoyed this,' Maureen whispered once they were finally seated with their beverages in front of them.

Aisling was tucking in to a wedge of lemon cake and poised with her fork. Roisin and Moira had opted to share a piece of chocolate brownie and they too looked up from where they'd been clashing with their forks over the last piece. Donal patted Maureen's hand and all three sisters eyes filled up, simultaneously missing their daddy but grateful for the hole in their Mammy's life Donal had helped fill.

'He'd have wanted us to enjoy it too, not sit around crying,' Moira stated. She was the first to get up from the table, victorious after scooping the last of the brownie.

'She's a good point,' Aisling said, polishing off her cake and following suit.

They entered the house through the main doors at the top of the steps leading up from the path running parallel to the gardens and as they began to explore found themselves awestruck by their sumptuous surrounds. Even the babbies were quiet, Roisin thought, but then saw Kiera was chomping on a rusk and the twins, content to be against their parents' chests, were asleep. There were gilt-framed portraits decorating the walls of the sweeping staircase depicting ancestors in wigs and the dress of a different century. You could smell the fresh floral arrangements peppered about along with the beeswax polish responsible for the gleaming timber tables, balustrade and floors. The furnishings filling the various rooms they crept into – because it was a house that inspired reverence – were plush with rolled arms or legs, and vases, tapestries and chest sets were on display. The different papers lining the walls of each room were works of art in themselves she noticed, equally rich in colour and pattern as any of the paintings she'd seen.

Quinn was reading from a leaflet he'd picked up. 'The house was used as a hospital during the Irish Civil War in the twenties.'

Roisin shuddered. She was trying to imagine the daily housekeeping involved with ensuring a house this size was spic and span. She'd not complain about the dusting and hoovering of her miniscule flat again.

'It would be Ita's worst nightmare,' Moira said, referring to O'Mara's Director of Housekeeping.

'This must have been a drawing room,' Donal said as they walked into a room dominated by a grand piano.

'Poppa D, I could play "Twinkle, Twinkle Little Star" on the piano there, I know how.' Noah pointed to it, eager to tickle the ivories.

'That would be a treat, Noah, but I think it's a case of look don't touch.'

Roisin's smile was rueful hearing the phrase every child loathed.

'It's such a fabulous place. I'll definitely be telling our guests to include it on their must see list while they're in Ireland,' Freya gushed as she admired a turquoise vase.

She was right, Roisin thought as they ventured up the sweeping staircase to see how the other half had lived. Bantry House was a treasure trove and a glimpse into the past.

The view over the lawns to the cannons at the bottom of the well-thought-out gardens to the bay beyond was magnificent and the three sisters gathered to admire it through the picture window in the bedroom they'd ventured into. 'Imagine waking up to that each morning. I wonder what it would have been like to have been one of the ladies of the house back in the day,' Roisin said.

'I bet they'd have got their breakfast in bed every day,' Moira said wistfully. 'And they'd have had a lady's maid to help them get dressed.'

'Would they have had to have worn corsets?' Aisling asked with a look of horror.

'Definitely,' Roisin said with the authority of a historian.

They turned to see Mammy behind them holding up the Magna Doodle on which she'd written: *'You three would have been no good in those days because young ladies had to do as they were told.'*

It was as their feet were beginning to say 'enough' when they found themselves passing by a gathered tour party in the entranceway they'd managed to avoid while exploring the house. They must belong to the coach they'd seen in the parking area, Roisin deduced, also noting they too were wearing matching tee shirts. Theirs introduced them as members of the Louisville, Kentucky Irish Genealogy Society. The logo was quite small given all those words.

A man in a cap with a camera slung around his neck and his jeans pulled up far too high to be healthy caught sight of them and elbowed his wife. She stared incredulously through spiky eyelashes at Donal then whispered to the lady with the big bottom in white capris next to her, who clutched hold of her husband's arm and repeated what she'd just heard and so on.

What was going on? Roisin thought, glancing at her sisters and Mammy nervously.

A voice carried over to them from within the party. 'Eli, honey, I cannot believe we've travelled all the way from Louisville, Kentucky to this here, high falutin' house in Ireland and who do we see but a country music icon from our very own home state.'

'I'd have thought you were out of your cotton pickin' mind, Marybeth, if I wasn't seeing him with my own two eyes,' Eli replied.

The woman in the capri pants tapped the couple on the shoulder. 'Kenny Rogers was born in Houston, Texas not Kentucky. You're thinking of Kenny Bishop.'

The spiky-lashed woman suddenly broke ranks and stampeded over to Donal waving a pen and clutching a little blue book. 'Could I get your autograph, Kenny? I'm such a fan. My favourite song's "Lady".'

Donal tried to explain he wasn't the country music legend but in the melee that followed he couldn't get a word in and, deciding it was easier to go with the flow, he began scribbling his name in autograph books and scraps of paper. If anyone noticed it was Donal McCarthy he scrawled and not Kenny Rogers, they didn't speak up.

While the others kept a safe distance back from the excited Americans, Maureen stayed steadfast and true by Donal's side.

'Look what Mammy's after writing on her Magna Doodle,' Aisling said.

They all looked to where she was holding the board aloft with the question, *'Would any of you happen to know what the secret eleven herbs and spices are for the Kentucky Fried Chicken?'* written on it.

'I hope she tells me if she finds out. I love the fried chicken.' Aisling again.

So it was ten minutes later the O'Mara Reunion 2002, party and the Louisville, Kentucky Genealogy Society tour group were treated to an impromptu a cappella performance by Donal of 'Lady' on the staircase of Bantry House.

Luckily he didn't bring the house down.

Chapter Thirteen

Roisin had been prodding her lip every ten minutes since they'd left Bantry, even though Tom had told her to leave it alone. The antihistamine had culled the itching, but so far it hadn't done much for the swelling. It was making her drowsy though Kiera, who'd been unimpressed with being strapped back into her car seat, was fussing, and each time she caught sight of her aunt's new look, her eyes welled up.

The novelty of the lush countryside they were driving through soon began to wear off, and the next thing Roisin knew, Tom's voice was jolting her awake.

'Claredoncally welcomes us, ladies.'

Moira, Roisin saw, was rubbing her eyes as she stared out the window. She did the same, expecting to catch a glimpse of village life. But, instead, there was still nothing but fields on either side of them. This did not bode well, Roisin thought.

'Ah, feck off, Tom, that's not funny,' Moira said.

The road ahead was empty, save for Aisling and Quinn's tank.

'We are officially in Claredoncally,' Tom protested. 'You'd not have noticed it yourself, given your mouth was hanging open and you were dribbling, but I saw the sign with my own two eyes.'

'I wasn't dribbling.' Moira swiped at the drool on her chin with the back of her hand.

'You were, and it was very sweet.'

They smiled at one another, and Roisin felt disgruntled. Thanks to that fecking bee, Shay would be rolling around in fits if she attempted to smile into his eyes like Moira was with Tom. She coughed loudly to remind them they weren't alone.

Her brother-in-law's attention was diverted from the come-hither gaze of his other half, but it was too late for him to miss the enormous pothole. The suspension scraped and groaned in protest.

'Jaysus wept. I hope Quinn didn't go down that,' Moira said, 'or we'll have you with the fat lip and Ash with two black eyes.'

Roisin wasn't listening. Were she and Shay cursed? She wondered, remembering their first date and the disastrous fringe trim that had preceded it. 'You're being ridiculous, Roisin O'Mara,' she told herself before glancing at her phone. Instantly the sun came out from behind the clouds because there was a message from Shay. It was short and sweet, but it was enough. He missed her and couldn't wait to see her and Noah tomorrow. Well, she missed him too, and banging back a message saying so, she decided not to mention her lip.

Maybe this peculiar mood she'd been struggling with lately had more to do with Colin's leaving for Dubai than Shay. Or, like Aisling was prone to doing, overthinking everything. She hoped there was a bar in this hotel Mammy had booked them into.

They rounded a bend, and a one-road-in, one-road-out village appeared. Claredonwotsit, she thought.

Aisling and Quinn's tank's brake lights flashed ahead, and Tom did the same as they passed by a church with its spire proudly pointing skyward. Then they rolled over a small stone bridge and into the village proper.

'Where's the tumbleweed?' Moira groused. 'And I'm sure I saw a net curtain twitching.'

She wasn't far wrong. Roisin's gaze swung to either side. The village wasn't exactly the stuff of chocolate-box lids she'd been hoping for, but on closer inspection she could see it would have been quaint once upon a time.

'Alma's tea rooms,' she mumbled through her thick lip to no one in particular.

A group of older women sitting by the window watched their convoy drive past.

'That would have been Great Aunt Noreen's shop once,' Moira said, pointing to the modern Spar convenience store.

A woman was tying a cocker spaniel to the nearby lamp post. There was a butcher, a pharmacy, a barbershop, a bookshop and a pub.

Claredonwotsit had good bones, Roisin decided, but it hadn't cashed in on the charm of painting the village shops in vibrant hues and prettying them further with hanging baskets. If she were on the village beautifying committee, she'd drape some bunting across the street too. You couldn't beat a spot of bunting. Still, she supposed the locals didn't feel there was much point, given their village was off the beaten tourist trail.

'That must be the hotel.' Moira pointed ahead to the uninspiring roughcast, two-storey building at the far end of the village.

As they drew alongside it, Roisin saw the sign "Isaac's Hotel" over the door. She continued with her prettifying Claredonwotsit theme, deciding it needed some greenery to soften the austere aesthetic. Conifers would be lovely, or perhaps ivy.

'Not exactly the Shelbourne, is it?' Moira said glumly.

'It's probably gorgeous inside,' Roisin lisped, trying to be positive.

Tom followed Quinn's lead and veered off the main street before turning down the slip road behind the hotel. The parking area for hotel guests was nearly full. Three trucks were parked on the slip road they'd turned in off.

Moira pointed at them. 'Rosi, look. Mammy's booked us into a fecking truck stop, so she has.'

'Speak of the devil,' Roisin said as Tom slid into one of the few parking spaces left.

Maureen and Donal nosed in beside them.

Roisin unbuckled the still-sleeping Kiera and then got out of the car, going around the other side to gently lift out her niece. Kiera stirred at the slamming of the car doors around them but didn't wake.

Aisling, carrying Aoife in her capsule, stood alongside her sisters. 'It's very utilitarian,' she said, shading her eyes and gazing up at the row of windows on the second floor.

'Ah, sure, it's nothing a few pots with some geraniums couldn't fix.' Roisin tried to put a positive spin on the grim building.

'It's like a prison, and we've all been sent down for the weekend for our crimes,' Moira muttered within earshot of Maureen, invoking a flurry of scribbling.

When she'd finished, she spun the board around.

'What does it say?' Moira was frowning at the scrawled words, pictures and symbols.

'I'm not sure. It's some sort of shorthand, I think. Although it looks like Egyptian hieroglyphics.' Aisling shook her head. 'Roisin, you're the one who works in an office. What does it say?'

Roisin squinted at the Magna Doodle. 'Okay, so I think, but I'm not one hundred per cent on this, MOM is short for Moira O'Mara. The fact it's in big shouty capital letters means she's annoyed with you, Moira.'

Maureen nodded heartily to convey Roisin had it in one.

Roisin continued to decipher the message. 'There's a letter 'I' then the word 'didn't', a letter 'C' and 'U' and a drawing of a hand. Is that a pocket there, Mammy?'

Maureen gestured, shoving her hand in the pocket of her Mo-pants, and nodded.

'Okay, so we've got Moira O'Mara I didn't see you put your hand in your pocket. So.' Roisin stared at the picture her mammy had drawn of a cake. 'I'm guessing this stands for shut your cake hole?'

Maureen gave her the thumbs up.

'That's lovely, that is, Mammy.' Moira pouted. 'And Tom and I are students, as you well know. We can't afford weekends away and the like. So you can't blame me for hoping for something a little more—' She shrugged.

'Charming?' Aisling supplied.

'Exactly.'

Donal, weighed down by bags, stood beside Maureen. 'Isaac's is the only hotel for miles, and the rest of the family are all staying here too, though how they managed to fit us all in, I don't know. Noreen said she was expecting forty or so, which isn't bad given the short notice she gave everyone. And she assured your mammy the hotel here is perfectly adequate. Besides, you'll only be using your rooms for sleeping, given all the socialising you'll be doing.'

'This gets better and better,' Moira sniped, taking the case Tom was thrusting at her and putting it on the ground. 'We're to be trapped in a hotel full of O'Maras for the next forty-eight hours.'

'She's never good when she naps in the daytime,' Tom offered apologetically.

Moira, ignoring her case, fetched Kieran in his capsule from the backseat of the tank.

'Christ on a bike, he's not one of ours, is he?' Roisin asked as a car belonging to another era puttered into the parking area.

They all squinted in the direction of the rattling vehicle.

'The fender's half off,' Tom noted quietly, pleased he was no longer the owner of the worst car in the lot.

The colour drained from Maureen's face.

'You've gone very pale, Mo. Are you feeling alright?' Donal asked, concerned.

Maureen shook her head, and Donal leaned over her shoulder as she began to write.

'Is that—' Aisling's voice, laced with horror, trailed off.

'Ah, Jaysus, I think it is.' Moira squinted for a better look at the driver behind the wheel.

'No, surely it can't be—'

Roisin didn't get to finish what she'd been about to say because Donal confirmed their worst fears as he looked up from the Magna Doodle board.

'Bartley. Your father's second cousin. Mo says none of you is to let him doss on the floor in your rooms and do not, she's put that in the capital letters, eat the cheese if he offers you any.'

Moira, Aisling and Roisin looked at one another fearfully. They all had memories of Uncle Bartley or Bart the fart, as they'd called him, because of his habit of breaking wind when he walked. Oh yes, they were haunted by his loud trousers and the stinky cheese he was partial to.

Bart the fart would arrive unannounced at the guesthouse looking for a free bed for however long the fancy took him. Mammy, who refused to let him stay in the family apartment because of his poor personal hygiene, would put him in Room 1. She'd then get about with a face on her for the duration of his stay.

On one occasion, he'd been with them for nearly four weeks when a stand-off between Mammy and Daddy had culminated in Mammy shouting, 'It's him or me!' It had been touch and go because their dad was a softie regarding family, but in the end, he'd put his wife first and had a quiet word with Uncle Bartley, who'd taken his cheese and slunk off.

It wasn't just Mammy who wasn't keen on Brian O'Mara's second cousin either. Mrs Flaherty had banned him from the kitchen after catching him cooking himself a grand old fry up more than once, leaving her short for their paying guests. And all hell had let loose after a bottom-pinching episode with Bronagh, whom Uncle Bartley thought was a fine figure of a woman.

He wasn't of Traveller stock, but travel from door to door, cadging a bed for the night is what Bartley O'Mara did. And, always, always did he have his lunchbox with the smelly old cheese with him. If he liked you, you'd be offered a wedge. If not, no cheese, and he'd stay anyway.

They all watched as a fella with a greasy combover who looked to be around Donal's age emerged from the vehicle. He wore a pair of mustard-and-red-checked trousers that would have made the Bay City Rollers proud. There was a collective ripple of disgust as he tugged at the crotch, sitting tight around his bits and bobs. He gave them a cheery wave, swaggering around to the back seat, where he fetched a bag and a lunchbox.

'Ah, Jaysus, he's still carting about the cheese?' Moira said out of the corner of her mouth. 'I hope it's not the same block he had the last time we saw him because I'm pretty certain those are the same trousers he was after wearing.'

'I wonder if it's blue cheese?' Aisling said to no one in particular.

'Don't even think about it, Aisling. Sure, Mammy will have your guts for garters if you let him slip you a cracker with the smelly cheese smeared on it,' Moira warned while Roisin pulled a face at Aisling, backing up Moira.

'Nana, Poppa D, come on!' Noah was not in the least bit interested in this Bartley fella. He was already opening the back door, eager to see what the hotel was like inside.

Not wishing to be accosted by her late husband's relative, Maureen hot-footed it inside.

'I'll give your uncles a hand with the rest of the gear first, Noah,' Donal called after him.

'Is he really as bad as all that?' Freya asked, wondering why she'd not heard of Bartley before.

'He's as bad as all that,' all three sisters agreed, telling her the nickname they'd given him.

'Eww.' Freya grimaced. 'I'm surprised Great Aunty Nono invited him. Well, I'm going to head over to hers now,' she said. 'Thanks very much for the ride, Quinn, Aisling. I'll see you all at the pre-dinner drinks later on.'

'You're welcome, and thanks for your help with Aoife and Kieran.' Aisling smiled.

'Ah, sure, they're wee angels, the both of them.'

Aisling smiled. They were, she thought, glancing down at her daughter's tiny face and across at Kieran.

Moira, who'd a tight hold of Kieran's capsule, kept Uncle Bartley in her line of sight. 'He's coming,' she hissed.

Aisling urged Freya to 'go now, while you still can.' Then, watching as the younger woman hurried off around the side of the hotel with her bag slung over her shoulder, she marvelled briefly at how lightly she travelled.

Quinn was busy unloading from the tank all the baby paraphernalia they'd been too scared to leave home without.

'C'mon, he'll catch you and offer you the cheese if you hang about out here.' Moira pushed past her sister, eager to get inside.

Aisling left Tom, Quinn and Donal to deal with Uncle Bartley as she followed in pursuit of Moira.

Roisin, cradling her sleeping niece, trod on Aisling's heels in her haste to get inside the hotel. No way was she getting left behind with Bart the fart.

They were all swallowed up by the gloomy interior. It was in sharp contrast to the glorious day outside, and, waiting for her eyes to adjust to the light, Roisin shivered.

Chapter Fourteen

Isaac's Hotel was, in a word, tired. The wallpaper, the carpet, the sofas for guests to sit on, all tired. The ambience wasn't helped by the lack of fresh flowers on the reception desk, the magazines on the occasional table being relics from the seventies, or the faint whiff of beer, cigarettes and old fat. Roisin turned up her nose without realising she was doing so. Noisy chatter drifted under a door to the right. She guessed that was the bar, where the first to arrive for the reunion were already gathering.

She migrated with her sisters to the front desk. Mammy and Noah were in the process of checking in.

The woman behind the counter reminded Roisin of a sandpiper with her sharp pointy nose. She informed them her name was Deirdre. Her head darted down to the reservation book, and when she looked back up, there was a suspicious glint in her beady eyes.

'She's looking at us like she thinks we're ladies of the night come to ply our trade,' Moira whispered. 'That's down to Aisling's tee shirt, that is.'

Roisin laughed, and Aisling deliberately trod on Moira's foot.

'Don't do that when I've a hold of your son!'

'It was an accident.' Aisling smiled sweetly.

Mammy looked fierce at them both.

'Here we are. I've four rooms booked for yer.' There was no welcoming warmth in Deirdre's voice.

'That would be right.' Roisin saved Maureen from having to write her reply.

'It's a clean establishment I run here,' Deirdre said, her eyes sliding from one to the other. 'I don't put up with any shenanigans.'

All four women felt their faces ripen to red. Roisin thought it was like when the customs man at the airport asked you if you had anything to declare, and you instantly felt guilty.

Maureen made a dry hacking noise, and Roisin was grateful she'd lost her voice; otherwise, they might all be out on the street.

'Maureen O'Mara! My dear departed cousin Brian's poor widowed wife. How long's it been?'

Moira muttered on her mam's behalf, 'Not fecking long enough.'

'Eh, what was that?' Bartley O'Mara held his hand to his ear.

'She said how're you, Uncle Bartley? It's a surprise to see you here,' Roisin, spokesperson as the eldest, informed him Mammy could not converse with him given she'd no voice.

'Would that be young Roisin now? Well, now, what a fine-looking girl you've grown into.'

He said the same thing each time he saw the sisters, and they all clenched, knowing what was coming next.

'C'mere to me now and give your old Uncle Bartley a kiss.' He puckered up.

Aisling jumped in. 'We're all not long after getting over a terrible bout of the cold sores, Uncle Bartley.' If there'd been a string of garlic and a crucifix handy, she'd have held them up.

'The mouth herpes,' Moira backed up her sister. 'They were all weepy and raw-like.'

'They're terribly contagious,' Roisin said.

'I can see.' Bartley winced, gesturing to his mouth. 'You've the terrible swelling still. Well, I'll just call into the bar there and say my hellos before I call in on Noreen to see if there's room at her inn for her dear cousin, Bartley.' He hurried off.

There was a collective sigh of relief and mass unclenching as the back door opened and Quinn, Tom and Donal staggered in with all the gear.

'I don't know what all the fuss is about,' Tom said as Bartley disappeared into the bar area, the door closing behind him. 'He seemed a friendly fellow.'

'It's not youse lot he's after trying to plant a wet kiss on.' Moira pretended to gag.

There was an impatient jangling.

'Your room keys.' Deidre slid them across the counter. 'Angus will show you up to your rooms.'

A man emerged from the shadows.

Jaysus wept, Roisin thought. It was Herman Munster.

Chapter Fifteen

Suzie plucked the silk dress from her case and carefully unfolded it before holding it out. It was a vibrant splash of colour in a bland and outdated room, but it was ill-chosen, she thought, frowning. She'd envisaged sailing into a grand hotel reception room when she bought it. Unfortunately, Isaac's Hotel was not a silk dress from a souk in Dubai sort of place. Instead, it was a glorified truck stop, and she regretted the exorbitant purchase, given that it wouldn't get a look in over their Irish holiday. She didn't know what she'd wear this evening. Nor did she know why it mattered so much that she fit in with Glen's family. But it did.

She hung the dress in the wardrobe and eyed her case, open on the floor. Ireland was not an easy place to pack for, given its reputation for four seasons in one day. She knew she'd brought far too many clothes, and all of them suddenly seemed wrong. The initial excitement of this special reunion had waned and been replaced by anxiety. What if it all went wrong, and she'd made a hideous mistake? Glen would never forgive her. Perhaps her wardrobe choices were a precursor of how this weekend would play out.

'What are you thinking?' Glen asked. He was stretched out on the bed with his hands clasped behind his head.

The rest of what needed hanging up could wait, she decided and, glad of the distraction, she sank onto the edge of the bed. 'I was thinking that you shouldn't have your shoes on, mister.' Her tone was glib, masking her mood, as she eyeballed his loafers.

'Do you think it matters?' Glen raised an eyebrow and made no move to kick off his shoes.

He had a point, Suzie thought. The candlewick bedspread was a becoming shade-of-fence-paint brown. 'Probably not. Is the bed comfy, though?' Weariness was creeping in. A nap would help settle her rattling nerves. She was tired from the flight, that was all. Everything would be fine.

'We're in for a serious case of roll together. It dips in the middle. That's not necessarily a bad thing, though.' He removed his left hand from behind his head to pat the space on the bed next to him and suggestively waggled his eyebrows.

It made her laugh despite the weariness. Then proving he was all bravado, Glen opened his mouth and yawned widely.

'My sentiments exactly,' Suzie said, yawning and then taking a moment to check out their room properly. Its only redeeming feature was the view over the fields behind the hotel. 'It's not exactly the Ritz, is it?'

'I don't think you're spoiled for choice in Claredoncally. I saw a B&B on the outskirts of the village, but that was it.'

Suzie slipped off her shoes and, pulling her hair free from the tie, lay down next to him. 'This place will become one of those amusing travel stories in months to come.' He was right about the roll together, she thought. It felt as if she were lying on a slope. She angled her head, expecting to see him smile his agreement, but his face was serious.

'Are you okay?' she rolled on her side, resting her hand on the hardness of his belly. He kept himself fit with squash and regular visits to the gym. She'd played the odd match against him, and he'd run her ragged. He was competitive by nature.

Glen was transfixed by the ceiling with its spidering cracks in the plasterwork. He was silent as he mulled over his reply, and the red digits on the alarm clock alongside the bed had flicked over by the time he spoke up. 'It's hard to explain, Suze. I expected it to feel strange being back here in Ireland, but I wasn't ready for it to feel so familiar. I might have left a long time ago, but it still echoes of home.' He turned his head toward her to gauge her understanding.

Suzie could feel his heart beating beneath the hand she'd moved to his chest and his eyes were brown in the gloom of the room even though the afternoon outside was bright. She propped herself up on her elbow, and the vulnerability on his face tugged at her heart. 'I can get that.' Did she dare mention his mother? The shutters had come down in the past when she had. What the heck, she decided. It was too late to worry about that now, not with what she'd gone and done. 'Ireland was where you last saw your mom, Glen, it's no wonder it feels like home. Because no matter what happened all those years ago, she'll always be your mom and Ireland will always be your home.'

His body next to her had stiffened, and Suzie held her breath. Had she gone too far?

'I'm a grown man, but sometimes in here' – he placed his hand over hers, covering it – 'I still feel like that nine-year-old boy.'

She blurted, 'I love you, Glen.'

He reached up to smooth her hair from her face. 'Suze, I love you too.'

'So don't shut me out.' A wobble crept into her voice. 'I want to understand what it was like for you.' She'd heard his mother's side, and he'd told her his father's side but the side she wanted to hear most was his.

He didn't look at her when he spoke. 'It's hard to talk about it.'

'You trust me, don't you?'

'Of course I do.'

'So, please. Tell me.'

Glen had been accused before of shutting out girlfriends. His relationships had floundered because of his inability to share. He didn't want to lose Suzie. He closed his eyes and the pain of the past welled up, and when he opened them, he found himself transported back to that fateful October day when his whole world had been upended.

Chapter Sixteen

♥

1972

'Would you like another scone there, Glen?' Rita O'Malley asked the young lad seated at the table next to her oldest and most troublesome child, Terry. She smiled fondly, seeing the crumbs down the front of Terry's school sweater, but it was swiftly replaced with a frown as she spied the split along a seam. A quick glance back at Glen and his sweater revealed his was in a similar state. She sighed. The boys had been tussling again. It was a small mercy that she'd not been summoned to the school to listen to the brothers' list of complaints about her son's behaviour.

Dara O'Mara wouldn't be called in to sit with her hands clasped in her lap, her head bowed, to be told her son was a wild one. Rita knew this because the donation Mr O'Mara gave to the school each year saw to that. They might be a pious lot with a short-term memory of what it was to be a young lad with too much energy, the brothers at the Sacred Heart School, but that didn't make them immune to hypocrisy.

Rita looked from Glen to Terry, noting how they barely had their arses on their seats. They'd be sore, no doubt, from the punishment meted out by the belt Father Peter was always quick to wield. She was surprised the girls hadn't tattled on their brother and his best pal the moment they got in the door. They were worried for his mortal soul, they'd tell her earnestly, and she'd have to bite back a smile.

Despite her consternation at Terry's inability to keep his fists to himself, there was also a sense of pride where her son's actions were concerned. Terry had confided a week or so back that it wasn't him who was on the receiving end of the name-calling that provoked the fist fights in the playground. It was Glen.

'They call his mammy awful things, and you have to stick up for your friends,' he'd said with wide blue eyes.

Rita hadn't known what to say to that, because he was right.

Her husband Dan wasn't keen on Terry keeping company with the young O'Mara lad even though they'd been pals since the first day of school. There'd been a change in Glen this last year, and when he'd been caught red-handed with the comic book he'd not paid for outside Brady's corner shop there on the high street, Dan had decided he was a bad influence on their son.

Rita would listen to him passing judgement as she mended his and Glen's school sweaters for the umpteenth time. She knew her husband well enough to know that what really rankled was how Glen's da, a solicitor who lived in a house twice the size of theirs, had managed to talk Mr Brady around. He'd smoothed the shopkeeper's ruffled feathers with the assurance it was an oversight on his son's behalf. He'd been so eager to read the comic that he'd forgotten to put the coins on the counter, and it wouldn't happen again. Dan was quick to point out that had it been their Terry who'd done the thieving and him who'd gone cap in hand to Mr Brady, his words would have fallen on deaf ears given his lowly status as a sawmill worker. It was the way things worked.

The chip her husband carried around on his shoulder must weigh him down something terrible, Rita had thought. What did class or status matter to a nine-year-old boy? She saw something very different to her husband when she looked at Glen. She saw a little boy crying out for attention, and the only way he knew how to get it was by getting into trouble. He was too young to understand it was the wrong sort of attention.

Glen O'Mara might live in a big house with furniture that wasn't on the hire purchase; his ma and da might not have to scratch around for money to pay the coal man or worry about the gas and electric meter ticking away merrily; she doubted his da worried himself sick about getting laid off night after night; and she knew Dara would never do the door-to-door for Littlewoods like she did. But for all that, the three O'Malley children were well-turned and well-loved. They didn't live in fear of what state they'd find their mammy in when they came home from school day after day. There was always a drink and a plate of something for their afternoon tea on the table. Rita liked nothing better than to sit and listen to them trying to outdo one another as they nattered about what had happened in their day.

This was why Glen was forever the fourth child at their kitchen table.

It was not so much whispered about town as shouted that his mam, Dara O'Mara, liked a drink. Rita wasn't one to pay much heed to the gossip, but, nevertheless, the story Silé Boyle had put about had reached her ears as it was spread through their small town with an 'oh how the mighty have fallen' glee.

Silé, a widow, had been on her way home from her sister's, who was also a widow, one evening early in the summer. The sisters would take it in turnabout to eat at the other's house of an evening. It was a mystery to most residents of Killybun why the pair of them didn't just move in with each other, but they steadfastly maintained their own homes. Silé had come across a holy commotion on this particular evening in the O'Mara's front garden.

'Is everything alright, Mr O'Mara,' she'd called over to the poor man who was desperately trying to pull his wife inside the house.

He held up a hand to signal it was nothing to worry about as he tugged at his wife's arm. Still, regardless of his assurances, Silé lingered a second longer at the gate to be sure.

At the retelling of the next part of her story, Silé would get a salacious gleam in her eyes as she confided things clearly weren't alright because Mrs O'Mara had begun to turn the air blue as, freeing herself from her husband's grip, she staggered about the garden in her dressing gown no less.

'What was the woman doing in her dressing gown at scarcely seven o'clock?' Silé would ask, receiving a disapproving shake of the head by way of response and a muttered 'disgraceful'. 'I wondered whether she'd bothered getting dressed that morning at all, given her unkempt state. And the smell.' She'd flapped her hand under her nose for effect. 'Like the Jameson Distillery, so it was. She could have bathed in the stuff.' The widowed woman would lean in conspiratorially then and say, 'Now you know me. I'm not one to tell tales, but I'm telling you now. Yer woman was three sheets to the wind. Worse than Paudie Shaw on a Friday night when O'Leary's calls time and sends him home minus his pay packet.' Before finishing, she couldn't resist adding, 'And her husband a professional man, too.'

Rita might have let this go as nothing more than tittle-tattle, but then there was the O'Mara's housekeeper, Mrs Grady. She'd told the bread man – who'd a tongue on him worse than the likes of Silé Boyle – that she'd had to help Mrs O'Mara up to bed before the young lad came home from school on more than one occasion.

Rita often thought it was an unpleasant human trait: this eagerness to believe the worst in people. She prided herself in trying to see the best in those around her and would have given Dara the benefit of the doubt had she not seen her in a sorry state herself.

She'd called around unexpectedly to see what could be done about their lads' penchant for getting into playground scraps. She had made the woman a strong brew and a sandwich to soak up the whisky she was after knocking back. She'd sensed deep unhappiness in Dara O'Mara, but whatever lay behind her drinking, she'd not revealed to her, and Rita knew she'd be wasting her breath trying to talk some sense into her. It was proper help the woman needed.

'Can we be excused, Mam?' Bridie piped up, interrupting Rita's thoughts as she polished off her milk and wiped the moustache off her upper lip with the back of her hand.

'We've to see to our patients, Mam,' Maggie, Rita's youngest, chirruped, her little face a picture of seriousness. The sisters were only a year apart in age and played well together until they didn't. It had been Bridie's idea to set up a doll's hospital fashioned out of an old crate in the corner of their bedroom with tea towels for bedding. And it had been young Maggie who'd wrapped toilet paper around the head of her favourite dolly, insisting she'd a bad head that needed fixing.

Rita smiled at her daughters. 'Off you go, Nurse Bridie and Nurse Maggie.'

Their chairs scraped back, and they clattered up the stairs. Then, seeing the plate of scones still untouched, she nudged it toward Glen and asked him again if he'd like another.

'Yes, please, Mrs O'Malley.' He helped himself to a half.

'G'won take the other half and eat them while they're fresh.'

Glen didn't need to be asked twice. 'Thank you, Mrs O'Malley.' He plucked the top half from the plate she was shaking at him and gave her a broad smile that lit up his pinched features.

For his part, Glen could sense Terry's eagerness to get outside to kick a ball about in the laneway that ran down the side of his house. But Glen was in no such hurry. He loved Mrs O'Malley's scones and how the fat blob of butter would sink into them, leaving a yellow pool behind. He loved how Terry's little sisters were annoying and would get told off for talking with their mouths full. He loved the smell of the dinner bubbling on the cooker top in the O'Malley's small kitchen as he wondered whether Mam would remember to put theirs on today. All she had to do was heat it up because Mrs Grady did the cooking, but she'd not manage even that most days. Most of all, though, he loved how Mrs O'Malley sat and listened to them all talk about their day.

Sometimes Terry would say he wished they could swap places so he could live in a bigger house with no annoying younger sisters poking about his things. Glen would have traded places with his friend in a heartbeat, but he thought Terry would likely want his old life back after a day or two. His house was silent, and he felt alone in it even when his mam and dad were home. The silence was preferable to the shouting, though.

'Before you go outside, give me those.' Rita gestured to their sweaters. She needed to crack on peeling the potatoes for dinner, but they'd have to wait. She wanted to get those seams stitched up before Dan got home and twigged there'd been another scuffle at school today.

The boys dutifully shrugged off their sweaters, knowing they'd soon warm up running about outside.

Rita took them from them with a sigh. 'It'd be easier if you lads would turn your cheeks the other way.'

Both boys looked sheepish.

'Thank you, Mrs O'Malley,' Glen spoke up, his face flushed with shame.

Rita caught sight of an angry scar visible beneath the cuff of his shirt. 'What happened there, Glen?' Her kindly face creased with concern.

He pulled the cuff down and wouldn't look at her as he replied it was his fault. He'd sloshed a pan of boiling water on his arm.

She stared at him for an age. For so long, he began to squirm under her gaze. Then she shook her head sadly before reaching out and chucking him under the chin. 'G'won with you, outside now.'

Chapter Seventeen

The lights were on in the houses Glen was passing by as he dragged his feet home. He'd noticed that the smells around you grew stronger once it was properly dark. For instance, the smoky coal fires burning hadn't bothered him when he'd been playing outside with Terry earlier. Now the smoke burned the back of his throat.

Mrs O'Malley, true to her word, had mended his sweater in time for him to wear it home, which meant he'd avoid another belting from Father Peter tomorrow on account of the ripped seam.

'It'll save your mammy having to do it for you, Glen,' she'd said with a kindly smile.

Sometimes he thought Mrs O'Malley must know how bad things could be at home. It was how she'd look at him. There was no pity in her eyes. Hers was one of understanding, and he knew, if he had to, he could talk to her about anything.

He'd almost told her everything he kept bottled up inside himself this afternoon. The words had swelled up, but he'd swallowed them down. Dad had made him promise not to speak about his mam to anyone, and you couldn't break a promise. It was very hard keeping all those feelings inside him to himself, though. Sometimes he felt he might explode like a bottle of fizz shaken before it was opened.

Not for the first time, he wished he could swap mammys, but then he felt guilty. His mammy was like Mrs O'Malley sometimes. Not knowing which Mammy he'd be getting when he got home each day was the hardest. On a good day, his mam would call out, 'Is that you, Glen?' from the kitchen as he dumped his bag and hung up his coat, and he'd hear the rustle of newspaper from the front room where his father was sitting waiting for Mam to call out that dinner was ready.

He played silly games, telling himself that if he stepped on a crack walking home, she'd be in bed when he got home. So he was very careful not to stand on any. Or, he'd turn his head to the sky, and if it were a full moon rising, she'd be in the kitchen singing while she served their dinner when he barrelled in. A black cat skittering across the front gardens on his route home was the best omen because it would signal a story at bedtime.

He'd very much like to see a black cat tonight. He loved those nights when Mam would sit on the side of his bed and tell him the story about the giant, Fionn MacCool, and his wife who outwitted the fierce, Scottish giant, Cucullin. He liked that story. Sometimes she'd tell him the one about the children who were turned into swans by their evil stepmother. It was a sad story, and he didn't like it so much, but it was worth listening to if it meant she'd sit on his bed and talk in that soft storytelling voice.

He stepped on a crack and froze. He told himself it was just a silly game, but a horrible sick feeling overcame him. Tonight would be one of those nights when he'd walk in to find his dad with his shirt sleeves rolled up, heating the dinner, with no sign of his mam. Dad would be overly cheerful in his greeting as he asked him how his day was, not hearing his answer. 'Your mam's got one of her bad heads again,' he'd say. 'It's just us for dinner, so go upstairs and change, son. Mrs Grady's done us proud tonight by the smell of this.'

Glen would take himself off, pausing outside his mam and dad's bedroom. He'd push the door open slowly, listening to it creak, and the smell as he crept over to the bed where his mam was sprawled would make his eyes water.

It was the whisky that gave his mam a bad head. Glen knew this. He'd found a bottle of the stuff hidden away under the kitchen sink and tried a sip for himself. It had made him gag, and had burned his stomach. He didn't understand why she drank it.

A snort on the stretch of grass between the houses across the road startled him, and he froze, forgetting about the crack he'd stood on as he strained his eyes. The shadowy shape on the grass, neither park nor field, just a patch of grass, belonged to Ned.

'G'night, Ned,' Glen called over softly, receiving a snuffling response. No one in town knew for sure where the horse had come from. He was just there one morning, much to the delight of the children of Killybun because Ned liked nothing better than being petted and ridden around the place. He thrived on the attention of which he was given plenty. Mr Thomas, the town's only vet, took it upon himself to make some enquiries, but nothing came of them. In the end, Ned's arrival in town was put down to the travellers.

The colourful band of travellers had set up camp on the outskirts of town last summer, causing all sorts of upset with the townsfolk who'd not wanted them there. It had been exciting times in Killybun so far as Glen and Terry were concerned because they were forever creeping about the edges of the camp, watching the goings on. Once, they'd even been chased by a traveller lad who looked like he'd give them a good boxing if he got hold of them. So they'd run as fast as they could into town, where they'd hidden behind the barrels stacked in the laneway alongside Murphy's pub. They'd not come out until they were convinced the coast was clear.

While the mystery of how Ned had come to Killybun had a satisfactory answer, the problem of what to do with him didn't. The townsfolk were not keen to face the wrath of the travellers if they returned looking for their horse to find him gone to the knacker's yard. It was common knowledge you'd be in for bad luck if you crossed them. So it was, Ned had stayed.

'Watch where you're going there, lad,' a surly voice muttered, and Glen looked up in time to see a man in an overcoat with an evening paper tucked under his arm sidestep him. He murmured an apology.

He was nearly home now. His steps were wide to avoid the cracks in the hope it wasn't too late to undo the damage. There was no moon in the sky tonight or black cats, although the yellow eyes staring out at him from behind the curtains of Mrs Brown's house must count toward something, he told himself.

His street loomed and, turning onto it, the house frontages became more extensive, set back from the road with expansive front gardens. They weren't all joined on like the O'Malley's house where you stepped out the front door and onto the pavement where neighbours congregated to chat. He saw the glow through the front windows and reached for the latch on the gate, but a funny thing happened, and his feet refused to budge. So he stood immobilised outside the gate until his knees began to knock with the cold. The puckered, angry red scar running down the inside of his forearm burned, and he balled his hands into fists to stop himself from rubbing at it. The doctor had told him to leave it alone, or it wouldn't heal, and he could get a nasty infection.

Mam hadn't meant to do it. It was an accident. She was trying to make him a boiled egg for his supper even though Mrs Grady had left tea for them like she always did. He'd been standing too close to the cooker, wanting to watch what she was doing. It wasn't her fault. The fuss afterwards when his dad came home had been terrible. Dad had made him stand with his arm under the tap, running cold water on it until he couldn't stand it any longer. Then, he'd shouted at Mam that she wasn't a fit mother while she sobbed sorry over and over.

Glen had had to go to the doctors and have the burn dressed. Doctor Richmond had asked so many questions, but Dad answered them for him, saying he'd got it into his head to boil an egg even though he knew better and, somehow, he'd manage to tip the pan up and scald himself. He was right. Glen told himself it was his fault. It was all his fault.

It was a cough further up the street that galvanised him to move.

He let himself in, his body tense, waiting to hear if his mam would call out. But it was his father, and tonight there was no smell of the dinner heating.

'Dad told me she'd had to leave to look after her sister in Canada.' Glen's eyes slowly refocused. 'I kicked off, of course, wanting to know when she'd be back, but there was this set to Dad's jaw when he said he didn't know, and I think I knew right then that I wouldn't see my mam again. In the end, I figured it was us. Me and Dad. We drove her away. For years I thought it was my fault. Suppose I'd not got under her feet. If the accident hadn't happened, maybe she'd have stayed.'

'Oh, Glen.' Suzie's cheeks were wet as she reached out to take his forearm, gently stroking the puckered skin beneath her fingertips.

He let her for a moment, then pulled his arm free and leaned over her to pluck a wad of tissues from the box beside the alarm clock. 'Here.'

Suzie hauled herself upright, took the tissues from him, wiped her eyes and blew her nose. People thought children couldn't handle the truth, so they sugar-coated things to make them palatable, but all that did was allow a slow rot to set in.

'It's ancient history.' Glen shrugged and rolled off the bed. 'I'm going to take a shower.'

She watched him as he pulled his sweater off, leaving it on the floor outside the bathroom and toyed with joining him but decided he needed to be on his own. It was all just so sad. But what he'd said about it being ancient history – that wasn't true. The hurt had never gone away. He'd said it himself how inside, sometimes, he was still that young boy.

She listened to the groaning pipes, followed by the sound of the shower and wondered whether Dara was here yet.

Oh God, she was going to be on eggshells between now and when Glen saw her, she thought as her stomach churned. Not for the first time, Suzie wondered if she'd done the right thing. In trying to mend bridges with Glen and his mam, had she sounded the death knell on her relationship with him?

Chapter Eighteen

'Nana said I can have a bowl of chips and a glass of lemonade,' Noah said, opening the door to Roisin before she could knock a second time. 'It's written on the doodle board,' he added lest she decided to challenge him. 'And that's where I'm sleeping.' The pull-out trolley bed he pointed to was at the foot of the double, covered in the same candlewick spread as the one in her room. 'You do look funny with your big mouth, Mum.'

'Thanks a million. And hello to you too. Can you not get it working then?' Roisin tossed over her son's head to where Donal was sitting on the end of the bed, jabbing the remote at the television.

Donal lowered the remote. 'It says they have the SKY TV, but can I get it working?' He shook his head.

'Ah, well, I doubt you'll have much time to watch it even if you manage to get it going,' Roisin replied to ease his exasperation.

Donal glanced over to where Maureen had struck a pose holding her new dress up against herself, waiting for Roisin's response. 'I think you'd be right there, Roisin,' he said.

'Is that new, Mammy?' Roisin knew it was a new dress and an expensive one, too. Moira had told her Mammy had been splashing the cash at her favourite clothing boutique in Howth again in readiness for the great O'Mara family reunion. She'd added that things were looking grim for the O'Mara siblings, with Mammy buying the cream cakes for Ciara with a C there in Howth each time she called into her shop.

Maureen nodded and stuck a leg out the side for effect. She mouthed something.

'What was that, Mammy?' Roisin entered the room, closing the door behind her.

Maureen's voice was barely more than a whisper as she relayed, 'It's a wrap style, very flattering so, and the colour is BO. All the rage this season.'

'Yes, you've told me that, both counts and it looks very well on you, so it does,' Roisin trotted out, glad Moira wasn't here to call her a fecky brown-noser. She was just glad the red silk, China Beach, prostitute dress no longer got an airing and the woman was putting her son up in her hotel room. Needs must.

Satisfied, Maureen hung up the dress. Meanwhile, Donal picked up the itinerary, and turning it over, he began to read out loud, 'There's drinks, and a mix 'n mingle down in the hotel bar followed by a sausage sizzle at Noreen's later.' He looked up. 'We've got to be there by seven. And tomorrow's breakfast, which is included in the hotel's price, will be served in the dining room until ten am. Then we've free time to explore the village of Claredoncally.'

'That will take all of five minutes,' Roisin muttered, thinking of things she'd far rather be doing than pounding the pavement of Claredoncally tomorrow afternoon once Shay arrived.

Donal smiled and carried on. 'A formal dinner at the hotel in the evening's planned, followed by entertainment. That would be me and, hopefully, Mo. If she rests her voice.' He fixed his gaze on Maureen.

She was reaching for the Magna Doodle.

'I reminded Shay to bring his fiddle, and at least we'll get a chance to get out of these.' Roisin tugged at her tee shirt.

'Don't pull it like so. You'll stretch it, Roisin. And do you want to dab the E45 cream on those lips of yours?' Maureen held up the board.

'You should have thought of that when you bought Ash a shirt two sizes too small,' Roisin mumbled as she shook her head in response to the E45.

Not quite catching what she'd said, Maureen shot her a narrow-eyed glower nevertheless.

'Mo and I thought we'd head downstairs with Noah shortly,' Donal said, standing up and stretching. 'She wondered if you could round your sisters up?'

Roisin nodded, remembering she was in fecky brown-noser mode. Besides, it was as good a plan as any, and she closed the door on the trio, saying she'd see them in the bar at some point. Then, padding over the loud carpet to the room she'd seen Aisling, Quinn and the babies disappear into earlier, she tapped on the door. Waiting for it to open, her nose wrinkled at the musty smell in the hallway. She thought it could do with a good blast of the Arpège-scented air freshener used at the guesthouse, hearing the mewling cries of babies inside. Maybe now wasn't such a good time. Roisin was about to move along to the next door to try her luck with Moira when the door was flung open. Aisling stood there with high colour on her cheeks. Roisin felt a dart of sympathy, knowing it was a sure sign her sister was frazzled. She could remember times like this with Noah when all she'd wanted was someone to march in and take him for a few hours. She didn't get a chance to open her mouth before Aisling held up a hand, stopping her.

'Before you ask. Aoife and Kieran are not hungry. I've fed them both, and they don't need changing either. They're tired, but I think they've twigged their somewhere different, which is why they won't settle. Jaysus, I'd have thought the antihistamine would have taken that down by now.' Aisling stared at Roisin's mouth.

Roisin ignored her sister's remark as, looking over her shoulder, she gave their room a once over. She returned a verdict that it was just as depressing as hers and Mammy, Donal and Noah's. But, at least, she wasn't footing the bill. 'And for your information, I wasn't going to ask.' Roisin hadn't forgotten how irritating it was when your babby was crying and people asked stupid questions like so, either. 'Listen, would you like me to take the twins for a walk? I might be able to get them off to sleep for you.' It wasn't an entirely selfless offering on her part because she'd relish some time on her own with her niece and nephew.

Aisling looked over her shoulder to Quinn, seated cross-legged on the bed with a baby in each arm, looking as frazzled as his wife. 'Quinn,' Aisling called over the top of their cries, 'Roisin volunteered to take Aoife and Kieran for a walk.'

'I love you,' Quinn mouthed to his sister-in-law.

Roisin grinned.

'That's a yes,' Aisling said. 'We left the pram downstairs in the back room behind the reception desk.' She moved aside to allow Roisin into the room.

Roisin honed in on the babies, with Quinn angling Aoife toward her to pick up. She did so, cradling her against her chest carefully.

Aisling unearthed hats and plopped them on both babies' heads. Then, as Roisin went to move past her with Aoife in her arms, she stopped her.

Quinn eyed his wife, guessing what was coming. 'Ash, Roisin is raising a son of her own. She knows how to look after a baby, and she'll be careful crossing the road, won't you, Rosi?'

'Of course, I will.'

'Noah's nearly seven, Quinn. She's rusty.'

'I am in the room, you know.' Roisin had been forewarned on the drive down by Moira that since giving birth, Aisling seemed to think nobody in Ireland knew how to cross a road safely. She braced herself.

'Remember, Roisin, look right, look left, then right again before you push the pram out into the street. And keep a tight hold of it at the lights.'

Quinn herded Roisin and Aoife out the door, a squalling Kieran still in his arms. 'I'll be back in a minute,' he said to his wife, shutting the door behind them and apologising to Roisin on the way down the stairs. 'She's a lioness when it comes to Aoife and Kieran.'

'That's as it should be,' Roisin said.

The din coming from the bar area was even louder than before when they reached the reception area, the wailing babies adding to it. Deirdre behind the front desk gave them a disapproving sniff, and Roisin wished she had Moira's gumption because her sister would have said, 'Have you not heard a baby cry before?' She, however, smiled sweetly or as sweetly as her oversized lips would allow and asked if they could fetch the pram.

Deirdre held the storeroom door open while Quinn wheeled the pram out with his free hand. He settled Kieran in, then took Aoife from Roisin, putting the baby boy's sister down the opposite end, so they were toe to toe. Then he fetched the balled-up blanket from beneath the pram and spread it over them, tucking it in either side. 'They liked to be tucked in. It makes them feel secure. And they like the ABC song. I used to sing it to them in the womb. Oh, and—'

'We'll be grand,' Roisin interrupted him, thinking that, at this rate, she'd never get out of there. Quinn was as bad as his wife. 'And I promise I'll bring back a pair of sleeping wee dotes on the condition you and Ash don't worry about them while I'm gone. Deal?'

'Deal. Thanks, Rosi, although I can't guarantee Ash won't worry. When I said lioness, she's probably more of a sabre-toothed tiger. I might suggest heading to the bar for a drink in peace.' Hearing an eruption of laughter, he added, 'Well, figuratively speaking.'

'I'll look for you both in there first.' Roisin began wheeling the pram toward the entrance.

'Rosi!' Quinn called after her.

She turned, looking back over her shoulder.

'You won't forget, will you?'

'Forget what?'

'Look right, then left, then right.'

Roisin couldn't tell if Quinn was serious or not. Either way, she flapped her hand in a shooing motion as Herman Munster did that mysterious materialising from the curtains thing once more and held the door open for her. 'G'won with you. Get back to your wife.' Roisin laughed, before stepping out into the sunshine.

Chapter Nineteen

♥

Roisin paused outside the hotel, tuning out the twins' wails as she stared down the main street of Claredoncally, where a few people milled about chatting or strolling along. She decided she'd mosey past the stretch of shops and then head back over the stone bridge they'd driven over on their way to town. There was bound to be a quiet lane nearby she could meander down and enjoy all that fresh country air. She was eager to soak in the ambience of village life because even if it didn't possess the charm of some of its neighbours, it would have a sense of community. That was what living somewhere like this was all about, after all.

There had been times when Roisin had felt very alone in London. Usually, on the weekends, Noah and his gerbil family were at Colin's, Shay would seem far away, and she'd miss her family. Sometimes, especially when she watched *Ballykissangel*, she'd imagine what it would be like to live in a tight-knit community. It had to offer a wonderful upbringing for children. There was that saying, after all, that it takes a village to raise a child. One thing Roisin had learned in her thirty-nine years was that you never knew what was around the corner. So it was with that thought in mind she pushed the pram along, daydreaming about herself, Noah and Shay living in a thatched-roof cottage in a picturesque village surrounded by countryside. It took her by surprise to realise there was another little person in the scenario she was visualising: a plump, smiling baby that was the spit of Shay.

Roisin had always assumed she'd have loads of children. Well, four, at least. So it had never occurred to her when she'd given birth to Noah that he might be her only child. She'd wanted her son to grow up with siblings to bounce off as she had, but things hadn't worked out like that. Colin had been reluctant to try for a second baby and, looking back now, she realised she shouldn't have been surprised. Noah wasn't planned, after all. He was their happy accident, although she'd never know whether her relationship with Colin would have run its course if she hadn't fallen pregnant. Her ex-husband was many things, old-fashioned being one of them, and when she'd told him he was going to be a father, he'd proposed, and Roisin, determined to give her baby what she saw as the best possible start, had accepted.

Those formative years had whizzed by, with Colin deftly changing the subject each time she raised the possibility of trying for a second child. Then, before she'd known it, Noah was starting school, and things had spectacularly unravelled with her and Colin.

Perhaps it was her destiny only to have one child. She should count her lucky stars. Sure, he was everything to her and wasn't she aunty to two beautiful nieces and a nephew? Was it greedy to want more? Because she did, she realised. She wasn't ready to give up on becoming a mammy again.

Nerves mingled with excitement as she decided to talk to Shay this weekend. It was the perfect opportunity to figure out what came next for them. Decisions had to be made because easy osi Rosi as her family called her, couldn't afford to sit back and let life drift by.

She didn't think about what she'd do if Shay told her he didn't want children. His lifestyle as an events manager and musician hardly lent itself to family life, but at least she'd know where she stood.

The cries were softening, Roisin thought. She was winning. The tea shop she'd noticed on the drive in was a few doors ahead. It was called Alma's and, as she drew level, she paused to look in the window, thinking how inviting it looked. The same women were still knitting with empty plates in front of them and a pot of tea centre stage on the table. One of the group looked up from her knit one, purl two and nodded a greeting to Roisin. You'd not get that in London, she mused, raising a hand in acknowledgement and doing her best to smile. The door opened, and a silvery head bobbed around it.

'Welcome to Claredoncally. You're here for the reunion, I see.' She pointed to Roisin's tee shirt.

'I am, thank you.' How perfectly lovely to be welcomed like so, Roisin thought, falling a little in love with this village.

'Now then, let me guess. I'd say you're one of Maureen's girls. Am I right?'

Roisin nodded, wondering how on earth she knew that.

'And given the twins there, you must be Aisling.'

'Not quite. I'm Roisin, the oldest sister, but the babbies are Aisling's alright. Aoife and Kieran. I'm giving Ash and Quinn a break by taking them for a walk to get them off to sleep. How did you know I was Maureen's daughter?'

The woman beamed, looking pleased with herself as her blue eyes danced. 'Noreen Grady's a good friend of mine. Of all of ours.' She was still holding the door open as she gestured inside. 'We meet here at Alma's every Friday and chat while we knit the jerseys for the little prem babies at the hospital in Cork. I'm Agnes. Noreen's told us all about you, and we've heard of nothing but this family reunion she's organised for weeks.'

There was nothing for it but to fib, so Roisin told the woman how excited they were to be here catching up with family they'd not seen in years.

The woman nodded. 'It is an exciting thing indeed and, I can tell you, Noreen was a different woman when she came back from your sister's wedding a few years back. But, of course, it was patching things up with Emer that did it. That girl's given Noreen a new lease on life for all her faults and the terrible time she and Malachy had with her. Sure, and didn't we all feel as though we were on our holidays with you listening to her natter on about the trip to Los Angeles you were after taking.'

'We did have a grand time in America.'

A voice drifted out of the tea shop, 'Ask her where she had her lips done, Agnes. Mine have got terrible mean and thin like in my dotage. I wouldn't mind a spot of plumping like so.'

'Don't pay any heed to Kathleen.' Agnes shook her head. 'She's never been any different. I've told her more times than I care to remember that a lamb's bleat is often more telling than a dog's bark, but she doesn't understand frankness is a euphemism for rudeness.'

Roisin had flushed at the mention of her lips. Sodding things and fecking bee, but then remembering the poor bee had lost its life due to stinging her, she took that back. 'I haven't had them done. I got stung by a bee earlier. It's an allergic reaction.'

'It was a bee after doing that to the poor girl, Kathleen,' Agnes tossed over her shoulder. 'So if it's the big lips you're after, dab the peanut butter on your lips and stand by the lavender bush in my garden. There are plenty of bees hovering about there. One of them is bound to attack you.'

'I wouldn't recommend it,' Roisin said. 'It's very painful, and I don't know how I'm going to eat or drink without dribbling.'

'She doesn't recommend it, Kathleen. She's after dribbling.'

'Well, it was lovely to meet you, but I'd best get moving if I want to get these two off to a sound sleep.' Roisin said her goodbyes and hurried off down the street.

She'd only walked a few metres when a woman around her mammy's age exited the hairdresser's with a perm so tight it would make a sheep envious. She peered inside the pram. 'Sure, you've double the fun there,' she exclaimed, straightening as poor Aoife's face screwed up tighter, and her wails started up again. 'Is it the wind? Trapped wind's terrible painful,' she bellowed over the cries.

'No. It's not wind. They're a little unsettled being somewhere new, is all. It's nothing a brisk walk won't fix.'

Roisin smiled through gritted teeth and made to move on but the woman blocking her path wasn't budging.

'Are you sure it's not the trapped wind? When our Hilary was a girl of sixteen or so, she's around your age now, in her forties like, she had tummy pain so bad we thought it was appendicitis. Brendan, that's my husband, God rest his soul, bundled her in the car and drove like the clappers, but before he'd even got halfway to the hospital in Cork City, she said she felt much better for having farted and that sure the bouncing through the potholes had done the trick.' She paused for breath, then stared at Roisin's lips. 'Hilary had her lips done too recently. She's forever pouting about the place now. Is it the allergic reaction you're after having?'

'It is, but it was a bee sting,' Roisin was quick to shout back, but she might as well have been talking to herself.

'A bee sting, you say. Well, would you believe the same thing happened to Hilary? The morning of her wedding as she carried her bouquet out to the bridal car. Terrible it was. Terrible. There was nothing to be done, and in all the photos the poor girl's in her wedding finery with a duck face like yourself. You'd have thought it would have put her off the big lips, but no.'

Roisin was already affronted by the reference to her being the same age as someone in their forties. Thirty-nine was her thirties, not forties. As for duck face, well, she spluttered silently. She was wondering, too, if the woman were a relation given the convoluted story she'd just told, because it was precisely the sort of thing Mammy would come out with. Although Mammy wouldn't use the word fart, that was more Noah's style. And, lastly, if she were poor Aoife with yer sheep woman's face looming over her, she'd be screaming too. It was time to make a getaway, but the woman pointed to Roisin's tee shirt before she could.

'You're an O'Mara, I see?'

Roisin was mentally cursing her mammy for the tee shirts as she nodded, before giving the woman a nudge with the pram. But she didn't take the hint, not budging.

'My Hilary's husband, Barry, his friend's brother is married to one of Noreen's nieces.'

Roisin thought she might have to ram her with the pram, but was saved when the woman spotted someone she wanted a word with. She watched in relief as her woolly head trotted off, yoo-hooing. Roisin didn't hang about, and just as the potholes had cured Hilary of the trapped wind, the bouncing over the uneven pavement settled Aoife.

By the time she'd passed the Spar, she risked a peek into the pram and, seeing two sleeping babies, felt inordinately proud of herself. She was so busy patting herself on the back she didn't notice the woman barrel out of the butcher's with a face like thunder until it was too late.

AN O'MARA'S REUNION

'I'm so sorry,' Roisin apologised, reversing off the staid brown shoes.

The little woman looked set to let fly, and Roisin reversed back a little further, knowing it was the small ones you had to watch. Look at Mammy, she thought. And sure, it was the same with dogs. It was the little ones who were more often than not feisty and eager to nip at your ankles. But then a miraculous thing happened. Roisin watched as the owner of the brown shoes' rabid expression softened upon seeing Aoife and Kieran. The peaceful sight of two sleeping babies made her forget her squashed toes. Babies were wonderful, Roisin thought. They brought out the best in people, and she watched as the woman smiled down into the pram.

'A double blessing,' she said, looking up at Roisin. Then, as her sharp brown eyes settled on the proverbial elephant in the street, Roisin's lips, she winced.

Kudos to her for not coming right out and mentioning them, Roisin thought. She decided she liked this woman as she agreed the twins were a blessing. But then, she remembered they weren't hers. 'They're my sister's babbies. The little one in the yellow is Aoife, and Kieran's in the green. I'm after taking them out for some fresh air so their mammy and daddy can have a break. They've just nodded off.'

The brown eyes squinted at Roisin's chest. 'What's that there on the front of your shirt?'

Roisin glanced down automatically, cringing at the tea stain down her front. 'Tea. I missed my mouth. It was before the bee stung me, too, so I've no excuse.'

'No. Not that. The logo there. I've not got my glasses on.'

'Oh! Sorry. It says O'Mara Reunion 2002.'

The woman morphed back into the terrier who'd had her bone snatched off her. 'You're one of Noreen's lot then,' she barked.

'Um.' Roisin was hesitant. She could hardly deny it given her tee shirt, but sensed to confirm this would be foolhardy. So she took the middle road. 'I'm distantly related to her, yes.'

'Well, you tell her from me, Maisie Donovan says her Timmy had his heart set on a nice sausage for his supper. And is there a sausage to be found in the whole of County Cork? No there is not thanks to that sausage sizzle she's after putting on.'

'I'm very sorry Timmy's missed out,' Roisin said.

She received a harrumphed response, then the woman looked past Roisin and said, 'Here he comes now. Sure, you can tell him yourself.'

Roisin spun around, but she could only see a cocker spaniel ambling toward them.

'Here, Timmy boy.'

The spaniel picked up his pace, coming to sit by his mistress' side, tongue lolling as he panted.

'G'won, he's waiting.'

So it was Roisin found herself apologising to the dog for the sausage shortage in Claredoncally. 'I'm sure if you swing by Great Aunt Noreen's, she'll toss you a sausage,' she said, seeing his woebegone expression before haring off down the street, eager to put distance between herself and the little woman. All of the villagers she'd encountered thus far, for that matter.

Her rosy notions about life in a village had been banished in the time it took to walk the length of the main street. Sure, you'd have to watch you weren't rubbing people up the wrong way all the time, and it would take you forever to buy a loaf of bread with everybody stopping to talk to you. She couldn't be doing with everyone knowing everyone's business either. It was bad enough having Mammy keeping tabs on her and offering her opinion on what Roisin should be doing with her life.

She spied a profusion of hydrangeas outside the rectory. And then there'd be the parish priest, she thought. No, village life wasn't her. But as she reached the stone bridge, she stopped and looked down at the water bubbling over the stony bottom. So, where did she and Noah belong if London was too big and a village in the country too small?

The answer was as crystal clear as the water flowing underneath the bridge.

Dublin.

Her home. That was where.

Chapter Twenty

Roisin hurried back to the hotel, the pram containing the sleeping twins in front of her. She'd planned on walking further and exploring a little of the countryside, but she was too keyed up by the decision she'd made to carry on and was desperate to tell Mammy. She needed to say the words 'we're moving home to Dublin' out loud. Only then would it become a fact.

The more she thought about it, the more it made perfect sense, and she couldn't understand why she'd not come up with the idea sooner. She'd been too worried about Colin telling Noah about his big move when they returned from this weekend away, she supposed. It had consumed her with worry these last weeks.

Her mind whirred at the realisation there was nothing to keep her in London once Colin left. Surely it would be better for Noah to be surrounded by family in Dublin. It would help take the sting from his father's going. He was young enough to adapt and settle into a new life, and it wasn't as if she'd be taking him somewhere unfamiliar. Ireland had always been his second home.

What about Elsa? Her internal voice whispered, causing a guilty pang. Noah's Granny Quealey didn't have much time for Roisin, but she adored Noah. She'd be heartbroken over both her son and grandson leaving.

'You have to do what's right for you and Noah, Roisin. Colin's doing what's right for him. Why shouldn't you? Elsa will be welcome to visit as often as she likes, and Colin will take Noah to London for holidays to see her.' She hoped Elsa wouldn't want to visit too often and then felt mean for thinking such a thing.

A man with a tweed cap pulled low on his head was sitting outside Murphy's pub, enjoying the afternoon sunshine. He puffed on his pipe, watching the woman push the pram past in a determined manner. She was mumbling to herself through a set of lips so thick she was putting him in mind of that singer fella his son had been a fan of. He shook his head and wracked his brains. He'd seen him on the television prancing about the place, moaning about not getting any satisfaction. Mick something. That was it. He smiled to himself. There was never a dull moment in Claredoncally, not if you took the time to sit and watch the world, he mused through a plume of aromatic smoke.

Satisfied that Elsa would be alright, Roisin turned her mind to her work at the accountancy firm. Her job was a means to an end. She'd find another, and she doubted Norman would shed a tear when she handed her notice in because there'd never been any risk of her being nominated for Secretary of the Year.

The questions kept popping up like scorecards as her mind whirred. What about your flat? Easy. The poky space she'd inhabited with Noah since Colin had lost their house was meant as a stopgap until... Until what exactly? Roisin had to think about that. To quote a turn of phrase, the likelihood of her ever saving enough to own her own home in London was as likely as pigs flying. Any extra money she managed to squirrel away went toward her yoga studio fund. The plan when she'd enough saved was to lease a space from which to run classes, but she could do that in Dublin. It would be much easier to make that dream a reality, too, with the support of Mammy and her sisters to help with Noah during the evening sessions.

But where will you live, and what about school for Noah? They have flats and schools in Dublin, you eejit, she answered herself back.

It occurred to her then that Howth would be a lovely place to live. Noah would love being close to the sea and his nana and Poppa D. She could set Mammy the task of checking out the local schools, and as for a place to live, it couldn't be as pricey as London. Fizzy bubbles popped inside her at the thought of her yoga studio. Mammy was bound to know someone who knew someone with something appropriate for her to lease.

Roisin reached Isaac's Hotel in no time, with the residents of Claredoncally giving her a wide berth on her return journey. The slightly manic gleam in her eyes as she chattered away to herself and having no wish to be mowed down by a pram had ensured a trouble-free trot back up the main street.

She was contemplating how best to open the door without taking her hands off the pram when that little voice said, And what about Shay, Roisin? What will he have to say about all your plans?

It wouldn't be right to mention any of what she'd decided this afternoon to Mammy until she'd spoken to Shay, she realised and the buoyancy of her mood was suddenly tempered. Would he be as excited by her plans as she was? And would he even want to fit into them? She'd find out soon enough, but right now her biggest concern was trying not to get pressed like a panini between the door and its frame as she attempted to hold it open and simultaneously wheel the pram back inside the hotel.

Chapter Twenty-one

'Glen?' Roisin stared at the tall, dark and handsome man descending the stairs who was vaguely reminiscent of a boy she'd known as a child. It was so strange how people stopped in your memory at the age they were the last time you saw them, which put Glen at nine. Face's didn't change, though. Oh, they thinned out, got fatter, older, whatever, but ultimately, you'd always catch a glimpse of the child they'd once been.

The man halted at the bottom of the stairs replying with a question. 'Roisin?'

Roisin nodded, a smile creeping across her face as he crossed the floor toward her. 'It's me, alright. A little older and hopefully wiser. Mammy said you were coming. You're so tall and—' she tried to find the terminology she was looking for because dark and handsome wasn't what she wanted to convey.

'Grown up,' he supplied with a grin.

'That's it,' she laughed. There was no trace of his culchie Irish accent these days. Instead, he sounded like a born and bred Londoner, which, she supposed, given he'd spent the bulk of his life in Britain's capital city, he practically was.

'And look at you.' He made a sweeping gesture with his hands.

'I got stung by a bee on my lips,' Roisin blurted. 'They're not normally this fat.'

Glen laughed, and it rumbled around the foyer. 'I did wonder, but I didn't like to say anything.'

'Good for you because everybody else has. So, Mammy was saying you're living in Dubai these days?'

'Yes. I've been over there for nearly ten years. It's a great lifestyle.' His voice trailed off.

It hit Roisin how one of the many lovely things about being a child was that there was never the need for polite conversation, and awkward silences didn't exist. She tried to channel her inner child but said, 'I was sorry to hear about your dad.'

'Thanks.' He ran his fingers through his hair, a flicker of sadness flashing in his eyes. 'I was sad to hear about Brian too. They were both too young.'

'That they were.'

A silent understanding passed between them.

'Mammy's with a new fella now. She calls him her live-in man-friend. Donal's his name. He's a retired plumber who plays in a Kenny Rogers tribute band, and he's lovely. Treats Mammy like a queen.' She didn't like to ask about his mam. Not after what Mammy had told her.

Glen moved the conversation on. 'So are those two yours then? They'd keep you busy.'

'They would, but no. Aoife and Kieran here belong to Aisling and her husband, Quinn. They're just over a month old. I have one son, Noah, who is nearly seven, and gerbils. Well, they're Noah's, technically.' She shrugged as if to say 'you know how it is' when she could see he didn't. 'His father and I are divorced. That was messy, but that's life, I suppose. Anyway, we live in London, but Colin, my ex, is after announcing he's moving to Dubai shortly like you. He's got a job he couldn't say no to. I've not told Noah his father's leaving London yet because I didn't want to spoil this weekend.' Roisin paused to breathe, realising she'd the verbal diarrhoea.

'That's, um, understandable.'

Roisin injected cheeriness into her tone. 'I've a boyfriend, though.' No, that made her sound like she was a girl of twenty, not nearly double that. She reworded her sentence. 'I mean partner. Shay's joining us at this delightful establishment tomorrow.' She quickly looked at the curtains to check Herman wasn't lurking. He wasn't, but a woman on the stairs was watching them intently. Roisin looked past Glen to the attractive blonde.

Realising she'd been spotted, the woman hurried down the rest of the stairs and headed toward them, smiling. Roisin guessed she was around her age.

Glen turned to see what Roisin was looking at and smiled. 'There you are.'

The woman apologised. 'Sorry. I couldn't decide what to wear.'

Roisin looked down at her too-big tee shirt and Mo-pants and wished she'd thought to team a baby-blue blouse with a pair of white jeans and sandals that made her look casual and put together instead of a sweaty O'Mara on tour.

'You look great.' Glen took hold of her hand, pulling her in next to him. 'Roisin, this is my better half, Suzie. Rosi and I used to get up to all sorts when we were kids, Suze.'

'Glen, that did not sound right,' Roisin admonished, giving Suzie a rolled-eye look that said her partner was a heathen. It made the other woman smile. 'What he should have said was we used to get up to shenanigans that had our parents pulling their hair out.' She'd decided to wipe the I'll show you mine game from her memory. 'My brother and sisters and I holidayed with his family a few times when we were younger. They were happy days.'

Suzie held out her hand, and Roisin took it. 'It's lovely to meet you, Roisin. Glen told me you all used to go blackberrying on the drive from the airport,' she said with a soft American twang.

Roisin gave her hand a gentle shake. 'It's a pleasure to meet you too. And we did. Your poor mam having to deal with all our clothes torn and covered in the blackberry juice.' Roisin laughed at the memory and then wondered if she'd made a faux pas mentioning Dara O'Mara. The woman had existed, though. You couldn't very well pretend she hadn't. Suzie put her at ease with her genuinely warm smile, and Roisin relaxed, deciding she liked her on the spot.

'I'm looking forward to hearing all about those shenanigans this weekend,' she said, and this time it was Glen rolling his eyes.

'You'll know all my secrets by Sunday,' he said, making both women laugh.

Roisin, remembering her lips, said, 'I got stung by a bee on the lip at lunchtime today. In case you were wondering why they're so enormous.'

Suzie looked momentarily taken aback and then winced. 'I wasn't wondering, but, ouch, I'm sorry to hear that. It must have hurt.'

'It did.'

'So, I know Maureen's here and Aisling, but what about Patrick?' Glen asked.

'Oh, don't be worrying about him. All he ever did was tell tales on us. Don't you remember?'

'I do.' That rumbly laugh echoed around again.

'And no, he's not. Pat lives in Los Angeles with his actress fiancée, and they're getting married next year. You'll meet Moira, though, and her partner, Tom. They've Kiera, who's nearly fifteen months now.

She's a character and keeps them on their toes. We all love her to bits and think Moira's after getting her just deserts.'

Glen's eyes were twinkling, listening to Roisin's lilting chatter. 'God, how long's it been since I saw you all? Moira was still in nappies when we left for London.'

'She was slow to take to the toilet training, but it has been a while. I make it thirty years.'

Suzie edged over to the pram and exclaimed, 'Oh my goodness, they're so beautiful. How old are they?'

'They're just over a month. Aoife and Kieran O'Mara-Moran, my sister Aisling and her husband Quinn's twins.'

'So precious,' Suzie cooed, her face soft.

'Aisling will let you have a cuddle if you like when they wake up.'

'I'd love that.'

'Do you have children?' Roisin asked.

She'd directed her question at Suzie, but Glen answered. 'No. Suze and I are foot-loose and fancy-free. Our lifestyle in Dubai doesn't lend itself to children.'

'Yes, um, work. You know how it is,' Suzie said, not meeting Roisin's eye.

No, she didn't know, Roisin thought, and Glen might see it that way but watching Suzie hovering over the babies told her she saw things differently.

'Were you going to brave the bar to see who else is here?' Roisin asked, changing the subject and warning them not to accept cheese on crackers from Uncle Bartley.

'I'd forgotten about him and his cheese,' Glen said. 'Does he still wear the loud trousers and freeload around the country?'

'Yes to the freeloading, although he doesn't visit us anymore, not since Mammy gave him short shrift. As for the trousers, they're positively shouting. And I can personally vouch for him still deserving the title, Bart the fart.'

Glen threw his head back, laughing at that.

'Well,' Suzie said, straightening. 'I, for one, am intrigued as to this colourful character. Shall we?' She gestured to the door with 'Bar' above it.

'There's strength in numbers,' Roisin said, wheeling the pram alongside Glen and Suzie. 'But remember, don't take the cheese, Suzie, and don't let him kiss you.'

Chapter Twenty-two

The trio were greeted with a din of chattering, laughter and the clinking of glasses in a more functional space than quaint. The smell of old beer and salty chips was pungent, but the smokers had spilt out into the beer garden for the children's sake. Roisin had seen on the itinerary it was a free bar until the sausage-and-bread supper at Great Aunt Noreen's. Judging by the rosy cheeks on display, certain family members were making the most of Noreen's generosity.

Roisin would have worried about the sudden noise waking the twins, but Aisling had told her that once they were asleep, you could do the Swiss yodelling next to them, and they wouldn't stir. She steered the pram over to a quiet corner and, as she did so, she heard someone call out, 'Well, if it isn't Glen O'Mara as I live and breathe. C'mere to me, lad.' And so it begins, she thought.

There was a muslin cloth beneath the pram and, fetching it, Roisin draped it over the pram to deter any O'Maras who might want to cluck over them. Then, she looked about the crowded bar area. Poor Suzie had been left standing on her own, with Glen having been pulled into the fold. Roisin made her way over and linked her arm reassuringly through the American woman's, because if she were in her shoes, she'd be terrified of this lot. 'I'll get us a drink, shall I? What will you have?'

'Oh, um, a white wine would be lovely.'

Roisin nodded and elbowed her way to the bar, meeting and greeting, not to mention fending off questions regarding the state of her lips along the way.

'I'll have a couple of house whites, please,' she called across the bar to the man with the broken veins of a seasoned drinker decorating his nose. Two generous pours were slid toward her, and she managed to carry them back to Suzie without spilling a drop which, given the jostling from the merrymakers all eager to say hello, was a miracle in itself. She passed Suzie her glass and saw her grimace as she took a sip. 'That bad?'

'White vinegar. But it always tastes fine by the second glass.' Suzie smiled.

Roisin raised her glass to her mouth tentatively. Given her engorged lips, it wasn't that easy to sip, but she was a determined woman, and she managed not to dribble. Shuddering at the acidic taste, she decided Suzie's verdict was spot on. Where was everyone? she thought, craning her neck to scan the lounge area and spotting her immediate family crowded around a table. 'C'mon, I'll introduce you to my nearest and dearest.' With Suzie by her side, she weaved her way over, informing concerned relatives, 'I was stung by a bee on the lips,' on the short journey over to the window table at which Donal, Quinn, Tom, Aisling, Moira and Kiera were seated. There was no sign of Mammy or Noah. That was no surprise. Mammy would be busy getting the writer's cramp as she caught up with faces she'd not seen in an age. She located her, showing a photographic montage of her Howth sea view to snooty Aunt Bernice, and grinned. As for Noah, he'd be high on fizz charging about the place. She could only hope he was behaving himself.

'The babbies are over there, Ash. Sound asleep with a muslin draped over the pram so as they're left alone.' Roisin was pleased to see her sister looking relaxed with a drink in front of her.

'I'll check on them in a minute,' Aisling said, calling across the table to where Quinn was talking with Donal and Tom to tell him Roisin had performed a miracle and got Aoife and Kieran to sleep.

Quinn mouthed, 'I love you,' at Roisin for the second time that afternoon. Then, Roisin did the rounds of the table, introducing them to Suzie.

Donal, ever the gentleman, handing Kiera, who'd a fierce grip on the flip-flop she was chewing, back to Moira, got up to find another couple of seats for them. He dragged them over a minute later, and Roisin and Suzie wedged in alongside Moira and Aisling.

Suzie gave the flip-flop a bemused glance before gushing over the twins and winning Aisling over immediately.

'I've counted ten "haven't you grown ups" so far,' Moira announced. 'And nine "doesn't she take after your Demi Moore wan". And I've had my cheek pinched three times by ancient great aunts. Oh, and one bottom pinch courtesy of Daddy's Aunt Margaret's second husband, Bill.'

'I'm up to eight of the grown-up comments,' Aisling said. 'And five "aren't you looking bonny on it" remarks. It's this fecking tee shirt. And four pinched cheeks, but my bottom's been left alone. Bill had a great conversation with my bosoms, though.'

'That would be six for the grown-up mentions,' Roisin added. 'And six, "well now I think it must be Maureen's side of the family you take after with those lips". No cheeks, bottom or bosom bother, though.'

'You wait. You've not been here long enough, is all,' Aisling said.

'It's like the torture, so it is.' This from Moira, who began explaining in great detail to Suzie why her daughter loved the flip-flop she currently had jammed in her mouth.

Roisin watched Suzie trying to keep up with hearing about Donal's fungal toe, Pooh the poodle's love of Donal's flip-flop and the rivalry between poodle and baby.

'Anyway,' Moira said, winding down her tale, 'Mammy's after buying new flip-flops for them both, so there's no tussling.' Her dark eyes flitted into the melee, and she nudged Roisin before pointing to where a beautiful young woman was accepting a cracker smeared with soft cheese from Uncle Bartley while Freya stood alongside her, smirking. 'That's Freya's sister, Keva, who's over from London. She does modelling. I don't think there's much love lost between them.'

Aisling, overhearing, added, 'Well, the salmonella she's in for will keep her thin for the modelling, at any rate.'

Tom put down his nearly empty pint glass and leaned over the table. 'And you'd want to watch out for the brother, Joey. He's a car salesman. They're never off duty. He's already collared Quinn and me and tried to do the hard sell on a second-hand Opel Astra. That's him over there.'

The four women looked to where Tom was pointing out a young man in an ill-fitting suit not much older than Freya. They watched as he whipped out his business card from his pocket and passed it to Aunty Maeve, who wasn't an aunt, but as with many of their family, they weren't sure exactly how they were related, but knew they must be given the shared surname. It was an unwritten rule that anyone older than them was automatically referred to as aunty or uncle, and anyone close in age was a cousin. They did recall having seen Aunty Maeve's ancient Morris Minor that she'd had forever and day in the car-parking area.

'He's picked the wrong woman there. Aunty Maeve will never part with Myrtle,' Aisling said. 'Not in a million years.'

Tom and Quinn checked out what everyone was drinking before excusing themselves to get another round in.

They'd need fortifying, faced with this lot, Roisin thought, watching them go as she gulped her wine so it didn't touch the sides.

Noah charged past just then, banging into the legs of Aunty Maeve's husband, Paudie O'Mara, who was already unsteady on his feet. He sloshed his pint down the front of his cousin Geordie O'Mara's wife, Fidelma, and when he attempted to dry her cleavage with his hand, he received a slap for his efforts.

'Noah!' Roisin called after her son, as another little boy ran hard after him. It fell on deaf ears. She shrugged to no one in particular. 'I tried.'

'What's it like being the mother of twins?' Suzie asked Aisling.

Wrong move, Roisin thought, knowing Aisling could talk for hours on the subject. She saw her sister take a deep breath before starting a sentence that began with, 'Well, I don't mind telling you...'

She had a rapt audience in Suzie, Roisin saw, as the American woman hung off Aisling's every word. What was the story there with her and Glen, she wondered? He'd been quick to say children wouldn't fit into their Dubai lives, but the longing in Suzie's eyes had been plain as day. It was a longing she was beginning to relate to.

Aunty Dara walking out on her son and husband must have left deep scars, she thought, but Kiera's grumbling cut off her train of thought. She caught hold of her niece's chubby hand and brought it to her rubbery lips, smothering it in kisses. Kiera giggled, and it was such a great sound. Roisin happily did it again and again until the little girl was in fits.

Tom and Quinn returned, placed the drinks in the middle of the table, and sat back down to begin a conversation about marathons. Donal joined in enthusiastically, having been a bit of a jogger when his children were young.

'Roisin, I was after reading how yoga's good for runners.'

Now they were talking her lingo! 'It is. It can loosen tight spots, strengthen weak spots and help prevent injuries.'

'Is it good for the stamina, though?' Moira interrupted.

'Very good.'

'You should look into it, Tom.'

Tom looked uncomfortable as he tried to figure out whether it was pacing himself when he was running Moira was concerned about or something else. He did not comment.

'What about for fellas my age, Roisin?' Donal asked.

'For the stamina?'

'No, for the aches and pains that are par for the course.'

Roisin felt Moira relax next to her and heard her remark under her breath, 'Jaysus wept. I don't know what I'd have done if he'd said yes.'

'It's fantastic for joint mobility, Donal.' Roisin banged her knee against Moira's, silently telling her to behave.

'I'd not feel comfortable tagging along to one of the sessions at the community centre there in Howth. Sure it's all full of women. It's a shame you don't live closer, Roisin, but maybe you could give us fellas some basic moves before you head home.'

Roisin felt that fizzy, pent-up excitement from earlier build once more, and she was about to announce that she might not be heading home for long when they all felt a shadow settle over their table.

'Hello there,' a stout woman of indeterminable years with more than a hint of moustache said once she had their attention.

AN O'MARA'S REUNION

Roisin half expected her to rattle some keys and say, 'Right, you lot back to your cells now.'

Instead, she looked at the three sisters for a moment, then said, 'Now let me see if I can get this right. You'd be Roisin, you're Aisling and you must be Moira.'

The sisters, who had no clue who this woman was, all nodded and smiled politely.

'I'm yer poor late daddy's third cousin, Aideen O'Mara. The last time I saw youse was at your cousin Darragh's wedding in the June of 1994. It poured down, so it did.'

'Yes, you're bang on, and of course, we did.' Roisin nodded enthusiastically, still not having a clue who the woman was. 'It's lovely to see you again, Aideen.'

Too late, she'd forgotten the golden rule. Aideen picked her up on her oversight.

'That would be Aunty Aideen, young lady.' Her attention moved to Kiera. 'What a pretty little girl you are.' She tweaked Kiera's cheek with her fleshy hand. 'My Molly and Kitty over there with those two gombeen husbands of theirs are yet to give me the grandchildren. I hear Maureen's after having four of them. She doesn't know how lucky she is.'

Kiera, who'd taken fright, was burrowing into her mammy.

'I'll take the wee dote for a walk about the place, shall I? Give you a break there, Moira.' Aideen held out two meaty arms toward Kiera. 'C'mon to your Aunty Aideen now.'

Roisin held her breath. She wouldn't put it past Moira to tell Aunty Aideen that Kiera had an aversion to moustaches, but before she could, Suzie came to the rescue saying sweetly, 'I've been promised a hold, first.'

The well-padded Irish woman and the petite American woman eyeballed one another in a silent match of first-to-blink loses.

Aunty Aideen lost and, making noises about suffering from the dry eye, moved away in search of other small children to hold. Kiera happily went to Suzie, burbling away. An enormous burst of wind erupted from her, making them all laugh.

'She takes after her mammy, there,' Tom said, raising his pint glass to his lips.

'Very funny.' Moira scowled at him.

Roisin glanced about to see if she could locate Noah, but instead spotted Mammy scribbling away on her Magna Doodle while Glen waited patiently to read whatever she was about to tell him.

Roisin pointed her out to Suzie. 'That's our mammy, over there talking to Glen. Maureen O'Mara, and just so you're in the know, like she'll be after communicating with you via the Magna Doodle as she's lost her voice.'

Suzie smiled over the top of Kiera's head. 'Thanks.'

Moira sipped her orange juice and, putting her glass down, said, 'You'll be looking forward to Shay arriving tomorrow, Roisin, although you'd want to be careful. The state of those beds, you could go right through them if it's the gallops you're after doing.'

Aisling shuddered. 'I hope we don't get bed bugs.'

'Oh, I think it's clean enough. You heard your woman yourself. It's a clean establishment she's after running here,' Roisin replied.

Suzie looked bewildered as the sister collapsed over the table in fits of giggles, and Roisin filled her in on what their hostess with the mostess had said to them when they'd checked in. She joined in with their laughter, as did Kiera, proving it was infectious.

'I think your mom over there's trying to tell you something,' Suzie said, gesturing to where Maureen was holding up the Magna Doodle.

AN O'MARA'S REUNION

'I hope you two haven't been on the sauce already carrying on like so,' Aisling read out.

As Suzie had predicted, Roisin feigned innocence even though the second wine was going down a lot better than the first. As for Aisling, she pointed to her breasts first. Then, she mouthed at Maureen, 'I'm breastfeeding,' before pointing to the juice in front of her.

'I don't drink,' Moira said. 'But, honestly, sometimes you feel like you're the only one in the world who doesn't. I mean, it's permanent for me, not like Aisling here.'

'Neither does Glen. So you're not the only teetotaller.'

'I'm looking forward to meeting him. But, unfortunately, I'm too young to remember him.'

'Well, I'm not,' Aisling said, pushing her chair back. 'I'm going to see if he can guess who I am.' Then seeing Kiera fidgeting on Suzie's lap said she'd take her with her for a little walk outside in the beer garden while she was at it.

The trio watched them go and saw Glen's face light up.

Right then, there was a surge for the bar.

'What's going on?' Suzie asked.

'The free bar's about to shut,' Tom and Quinn said, getting up and joining the swell of thirsty O'Maras.

Chapter Twenty-three

The sky was washed pale blue as the O'Mara clan exited Isaac's Hotel to find themselves blinking in the fresh air. The evening was fine and warm, which given the sausage sizzle would presumably be in Great Aunt Noreen's garden, was a blessing, Roisin thought, setting off with the rest of her family. Freya and her siblings took the lead as they knew the quickest way to the little house their mam shared on the edge of the village with their Great Aunt Nono.

'We won't stay late, Mammy,' Aisling said as she walked alongside Maureen and Donal. On her other side, Quinn pushed the pram with the twins, who were now awake and would soon announce they needed feeding. 'We'll say our hellos and have dinner, then head back to the hotel.'

'The same with us, Mammy,' Moira said as Kiera, thumb in mouth, sat quietly in her pushchair. 'It's been a big day.'

Maureen did not comment other than nod.

Roisin yawned. It was the culmination of a day in the car, momentous decision-making and the three wines she'd knocked back.

Nothing was stopping her from kicking up her heels, given Mammy and Donal would be taking Noah back to the hotel with them tonight, though. Nothing but the thought of fending off Uncle Bill and Uncle Bartley. No, thank you, she thought to herself. Besides, she wanted to be in good form tomorrow when Shay arrived. She needed a clear head to find the right words and the courage to say what she'd decided needed to be said.

'It's very quiet,' Donal remarked.

'It's strange when you're used to busy streets,' Aisling said, then lowered her voice. 'The curtains are twitching, look.'

Their little procession glanced to the rows of higgledy-piggledy houses where the curtains were twitching.

'To be fair, I don't suppose it's every day forty or so people go marching down their street in search of sausages and bread,' Roisin said.

'It's like the twilight zone,' Moira whispered, rubbing at her arms, which had gone goosey.

They all jumped as a tabby cat sat on the front doorstep of a row of houses they were passing by miaowed loudly.

'At least he's not a black cat,' Aisling said, shuffling closer to Quinn.

Maureen firmly linked her arm through Donal's, and Moira wrapped herself around Tom.

'I quite like it. It's very peaceful,' Roisin said.

All eyes swung her way in disbelief. 'But you live in London,' they exclaimed incredulously.

'That doesn't mean I don't appreciate getting out of the rat race.' She said nothing more on the subject because it had occurred to her while sitting in the noisy hotel bar that she wouldn't be able to share the news that she and Noah would be moving back to Dublin until after Colin had spoken to their son upon their return to London. So much change was coming her little boy's way, she thought, looking to where he was half walking, half skipping along with the little friend he'd made a little ways ahead. How would he cope with it all?

'You look a million miles away there, Rosi, penny for them?' Donal said, a twinkle in his eye. 'Are you imagining yourself, Noah and Shay in a quiet, cosy country cottage by any chance?'

'Is she my arse,' Moira interrupted. 'As Mammy would say, Rosi's mind will be in the gutter. Oh, she'll have Shay on the brain alright because she always gets that daft look on her face when she's seeing him.'

'Ah, absence makes the heart grow fonder,' Donal said poetically.

Maureen looked up at him adoringly.

Roisin smiled, happy to play along as she told Donal she was looking forward to seeing Shay tomorrow.

'It will be grand to see him and I hope you reminded him to bring his fiddle.'

'He'll be fiddling, alright,' Moira snickered.

Maureen glared, and the internal debate as to whether she held them all up while she wrote on the Magna Doodle that Moira was to shut her mouth or she'd redden her arse was plain for all to see. But, in the end, the glare had to suffice. She didn't want to be responsible for them missing out on the sausages because the others had cleaned them out before they arrived.

'He is bringing his fiddle Donal,' Roisin assured him, aiming a kick at Moira's shins as, unable to help herself, she'd muttered, 'I bet he is. He'll probably have bells on it.'

Maureen tugged on Donal's arm. He bent his head close to hers to catch what she wanted to say.

'Your mammy says you're not to forget she's a spare tee shirt for Shay, and she'll swing for you in a minute, Moira.'

'I won't forget,' Roisin said as Tom told Moira to behave.

A little ways ahead, she could see Glen and Suzie. They were strolling hand in hand. It was lovely Glen had found someone like Suzie, but she hoped he didn't lose her over his evident reticence toward starting a family. As she'd find out herself soon enough, it was a deal-breaker for some couples. Mind you, seeing his family genetics gathered en masse like so might make Suzie think twice about babies, she thought, watching Uncle Bartley pull his trousers out of his arse crack.

Jaysus wept. What would Shay make of them all? She couldn't be worrying about that, though. Instead, she recalled how Suzie had confided she was unsure about the dress she'd brought with her from Dubai for tomorrow evening's more formal dinner at the hotel.

'I'm worried it might seem a little over the top,' she'd said.

Roisin had smiled and told her there was no such thing as being over the top in her family.

A car pootled past and tooted a greeting, receiving a beery cheer and wave, and the twilight zone was forgotten as much chatter about how friendly people were in the country ensued and how you'd never get a greeting like that in the big smoke.

Claredoncally was only a tiny place, and Great Aunt Noreen's house was set three streets back from the village shops down what Roisin assumed would generally be a quiet lane. A smattering of newish dwellings were laid out on one side, and on the other a low hedge separated cultivated fields, which gave way to undulating hills with the odd craggy outcrop in the distance. The vista was magnificent and stretched as far as the eye could see.

As they drew closer to their destination, they caught a teasing whiff of frying sausages and onions. It had noses twitching, and there was a collective sigh of relief when ten or so steps later they came to a newish brick house and, following the others, trooped single file down the side path. They'd have been able to find the place by a sense of smell alone, Roisin thought, her stomach grumbling at the prospect of sustenance to mop up those wines.

'That's a smell that should be bottled,' Aisling said, belly-inhaling appreciatively, and Roisin nodded her agreement.

Given the size of the house, the garden was surprisingly large and perfectly able to accommodate the gathering beginning to fill it. A white marquee without sides had been erected on the grassy area between the riotous flower beds framing the fence line, and Roisin spotted three garden gnomes peeking out at them from the foliage.

She caught up to Noah and tapped him on the shoulder. 'I spy with my little eye something beginning with G.'

She laughed when he shouted a few seconds later, causing one or two of the older folk standing nearby to jump, 'Garden gnomes!'

'Well done.' She ruffled his hair and planted a kiss on top of his head. His Granny Quealey had several in her garden which he'd named.

A long trestle table had been set up under the marquee upon which condiments like tomato sauce, mustard, salt and pepper, and serviettes were laid down on one end. Drinks filled the other end. It was surprising the whole thing didn't topple over, given how heavy the drinks end was, Roisin thought. Two girls of about sixteen or so were standing behind the makeshift bar pouring drinks into plastic cups like seasoned pros, and sausages were being turned on the BBQ, which Freya had told them Great Aunt Nono had hired for the evening, by a lad in his teens. Another lad around the same age as the cook was frantically buttering bread. According to Freya, they'd been roped in by the local youth group who were saving for a trip to France next year.

Plastic chairs were set out in clusters about the garden, and Aisling announced she needed to feed the twins as she made for one of the chairs. Quinn followed behind her, bumping the pram across the grass.

Mammy and the Magna Doodle made a beeline for Noreen, who was milling about overseeing the youngsters charged with ensuring everyone was fed and watered. She looked very well in her colourful floaty emerald-green dress. Emer, Roisin saw casting about the garden, was trying to dislodge herself from a soft patch of soil into which her heels had sunk. Roisin gave Moira a surreptitious nudge, and they smirked, watching her rock back and forth in an outfit that was far too young for her to free herself. Eventually, she staggered forth.

'She looks like a stork in those heels. I wouldn't say it if she were nice, but poor Freya having her for a mammy,' Moira whispered.

'You can't pick your family,' Roisin whispered back.

They both looked to Uncle Bartley, sitting in a chair with his cheese-and-cracker container tucked underneath it. He had a sausage lying on a piece of bread in each hand and a plastic cup of beer balanced on the grass alongside him. Someone turned the music up a notch, and it had his feet tapping. To Roisin's ears, it sounded suspiciously like Foster & Allen. She thought they'd all be linking arms and swaying to 'Maggie' in no time.

Donal tagged onto the end of the queue for a sausage with Noah, and Moira moved to follow, saying, 'C'mon, we better get in there too, or there'll be none left. This lot are gannets.'

'I was going to say hello to Great Aunt Noreen first,' Roisin said.

'Sure, there's plenty of time for that once we've eaten.'

She was right and, besides, she was starving, Roisin thought.

'I think Aisling's trying to get your attention.' Tom pointed out their sister.

Roisin and Moira looked to where Aisling was mouthing something over at them. Kieran was already in the crook of her left arm, and

Quinn was lifting Aoife from the pram. Aisling held up two fingers when she saw she had their attention.

'Why's she doing the fingers like so?' Tom asked. 'Your mammy won't be happy.'

'It's not the fingers, you eejit.' Moira laughed. 'She wants us to get her two sausages, though how she thinks she'll eat them given her hands are full, I don't know.'

'If anyone can find a way, it's our Ash,' Roisin said, and she and Moira laughed.

They inched forward in the line.

'How will Kiera go with a sausage?' Roisin looked at her niece, who was now on high alert in her pram, ready for dinner.

'She'll make short work of it,' Moira said. 'The trick will be making sure she doesn't jam the whole thing in her gob before I can break it into pieces for her. She takes after her Aunty Aisling when it comes to her food.'

'What traits of mine does she have?' Roisin asked, not wanting to be left out.

'Well, she's very fond of that pose you call the happy baby. You know where you lie on your back and grab hold of your toes. And she likes the one where you get on all fours then raise your arse in the air, too.'

Roisin smiled. 'Downward dog. She's a yoga baby.' What Moira had just said gave her an idea for her studio when she opened it. Classes for toddlers. She was sure they'd be a hit. Then there was what Donal said back at the hotel earlier about not feeling comfortable joining the local yoga classes as the only male. Why couldn't she run courses exclusively for the menfolk too? Her mind buzzed because she was sure there'd be a market for both.

'Who's that Suzie and Glen are after talking to?' Moira was asking. 'I didn't see him earlier, but he's familiar.'

Roisin located the couple near the trestle table. 'That's because he's a relative, you eejit.' At second glance, though, she realised it was their loosely related cousin, Reuben. 'I remember him. Reuben's his name. He had a terrible tantrum at the family picnic held in Wicklow one summer when he kept missing the ball during the game of rounders. It was like watching a young John McEnroe in action, so it was.'

It didn't take long for them to reach the business end of the line, and after a tussle with Kiera over the sausage she'd tried to snatch and grab off her mammy, they moseyed over to join Aisling and Quinn. Noah took off to join his friend, and Donal carried two paper plates over to where Maureen was still chatting with Noreen.

There wasn't a sound as they ate, enjoying the evening sun's warmth. Tom, the first to finish, wiped his hands on a napkin and sorted out drinks for everyone while Roisin and Moira amused themselves watching Quinn, who was still hand-feeding Aisling. They agreed it was great craic, especially when Aisling upped the ante by nearly taking off Quinn's fingers as she ate the last sausage.

'I'm still hungry,' Moira said once she'd stopped laughing. She looked over at the barbeque. 'Oh, good, there's more being cooked.'

Roisin glanced over in time to see a new bag of sausages being tipped on the hot plate. She'd be having seconds too. Aisling was already placing her order with Quinn.

'C'mon, Rosi, let's go up now before any of the others get in there,' Moira said.

The two sisters had just stood up when a blanket-like hush settled over the boisterous alfresco family gathering.

'What's going on?' Quinn asked.

'Who's that?' Moira asked, seeing the cause of the sudden stillness.

A woman was standing on the path at the garden's edge, her hands clasped in front of her as she anxiously scanned the gathered faces.

It took Roisin a moment or two to place her, but then she clicked, and her heart shot up into her mouth.

'Oh, Jaysus. It's Glen's mam, Dara.'

Chapter Twenty-four

You could have heard a pin drop if it weren't for Foster & Allen, Roisin thought, and then the comments began to fly about the garden as the realisation dawned as to who the unexpected guest was.

Roisin caught the phrase 'brass neck' muttered. She didn't know about that. Brave was the word that sprang to mind seeing the poor woman, waif-like in her green sundress, standing there like an accused witch about to stand trial.

Dara, her silvered hair in a loose bun, was the same age, more or less as Mammy, but her face told another story, Roisin thought, dragging her eyes away to seek out Glen. Did he know his mam was going to be here? If not, then he'd have just had an awful shock.

Glen and Suzie hadn't moved from where they'd been standing alongside the marquee. It was apparent from the way the colour had leached from his face he'd no clue his mother was going to be there.

Dara took a hesitant step toward her son, but his expression stopped her. Meanwhile, Suzie had gripped his forearm, and her lips were moving urgently as she conveyed something to him. Roisin tried to read the situation, which became evident as Glen shook himself free from his girlfriend's grasp. Whatever Suzie had been saying, he didn't want to hear it. The shock was visible in his pallor, but the anger was in his clenched hands.

Glen suddenly said in a voice loud enough to carry, 'You had no right!' Then without a glance back at Suzie or the woman he'd called mam for the first nine years of his life, he strode from the garden.

Dara's shoulder's slumped, and Suzie stood statue-like for a moment before shaking herself out of it. She made to go after him, apologising to Dara, who called after her not to go. Suzie's step faltered.

'Jaysus wept, it wouldn't be a family get-together without some sort of drama, but this is more edge of your seat than when they do the *Big Brother* evictions,' Moira said.

'Shut up, Moira,' Roisin said, unable to stand there doing nothing. She crossed the lawn to where the two women were talking earnestly. 'Suzie, Aunty Dara,' she interrupted. 'I'm not sure what's going on, but you don't need this lot gawping at you. C'mon, we'll go back to the hotel and see if we can't fetch you a cup of tea.' She didn't know why she'd suggested tea, other than it was what Mammy always rolled out in times of crisis.

She felt someone touch her elbow then and, as though she'd rubbed the magic genie bottle, there was the woman herself.

Maureen cut to the chase, using what was left of her voice to say, 'It's been a long time, Dara. Am I to take it Glen had no clue you'd be here?' Her tone was neutral. Neither warm and welcoming nor frosty and standoffish.

'This is my fault,' Suzie said, her eyes glistening and her bottom lip trembling as she twisted her hands together, trying to maintain her composure. 'I suggested Dara come. She's travelled from Canada for nothing. I'm sorry, Dara. I thought he'd at least hear you out.' She bit down on her lip. 'I've never seen him like that before. What should I do?' She looked to each of the women, not waiting for an answer. 'I want to go after him, to try to talk to him, but I don't know. I've never seen him so angry.'

Dara put a comforting arm around her shoulder, pulling her to her. 'It's not your fault, Suzie. You tried, and I'm grateful. It's me the blame lies with. No one else.'

Roisin listened to her soft accent, an unusual mix of Irish and Canadian. There would be time for recriminations and sorry later, but it was Glen she was worried about right now. Should she try to catch him up? Would he want the cousin he'd not seen since he was a child poking her nose in, though?

'I think you should go after Glen, Roisin,' Maureen managed to gasp, putting Roisin's thoughts into words.

She should, yes. She nodded, confirming this to herself as much as the others. What if he went back to the hotel and drove off someplace? The cocktail of shock mixed with drinking could be a lethal combination behind the wheel.

Noreen joined their huddle, taking charge. 'Hello, Dara. Listen to me now. Why don't you and Suzie come inside with myself and Maureen? I'll put the kettle on, or I have a drop of the good stuff tucked away because I'll not be wasting it on this lot.' She eyed her still-curious extended family.

Dara looked gratefully at Noreen. 'Tea will be fine. Thank you, Noreen. I've not touched a drop in thirty years.'

'Good for you,' Noreen said.

Roisin was already walking away when Dara called after her, 'Roisin, if you catch Glen up will you tell him I came to tell him I'm sorry for what happened.'

'I'm sorry too,' Suzie's voice shook.

Roisin didn't get a chance to say she would because Dara and Suzie were already being swept inside the house by Noreen and Maureen.

Roisin saw Glen ahead, striding in the opposite direction of the hotel. At least he'd had the sense not to consider driving, she thought. The lane circled around, presumably back to the village, and he was nearly out of her line, so she set off at a jog. It wasn't long before she was puffing and wishing she had time to slot some cardio into her daily routine. The gap between them began to lessen with each step, though.

As she drew closer, he must have sensed someone behind him because he turned around and saw his red-faced cousin approaching. He shoved his hands in his pockets and waited. When she reached him, she put her hands on her knees and tried to catch her breath. Glen's face was stony when she straightened and pushed her hair back from her sticky face.

'I know you probably want to be on your own, but I wanted to make sure you were alright.'

Glen shrugged. 'I'm not, but I will be. Don't worry about me, Roisin. You go back to the party. I need to clear my head. It was a shock seeing her there like that.'

'I can imagine.'

There was no sound other than cows lowing in the fields behind the hedgerow. He began to walk on, expecting Roisin to turn and go back in the direction she'd come, but she walked alongside him.

'I can't get rid of you?' He raised a brow, his half smile taking the bite from his words.

'I'm channelling Aisling. Don't you remember how she'd insist on joining in with whatever we were planning to play even though I'd tell her to clear off?'

Glen managed a laugh. 'Kids can be cruel.'

'So can adults,' Roisin said softly.

Glen's voice cracked as he said, 'You're not wrong there. I can't believe Suzie would go behind my back like so. She knows what happened. You're a mother yourself, Roisin. You tell me, could you imagine leaving Noah and never having contact with him again? I mean, what was Suzie thinking?'

'I don't know the ins and outs of it all, Glen, but I know Suzie loves you. And you love her. She'd not have contacted Aunty Dara unless she thought it would help you.'

'You've no clue what happened back then, have you?' Glen's eyes were fixed firmly on the road ahead.

'We were told your mam had gone to Canada to look after her sick sister, and it was never mentioned again. I thought your mam's sister must be very sick, which is why she didn't come back. You accept what you're told when you're a child.'

Glen looked at her oddly. 'Dad told me Mam was sick and had to go away and that it wasn't likely she'd be coming back. My father was a good man, but I knew when not to press him and where my mam was concerned, after she'd gone, he drew a line under her ever having been in our lives.'

'You moved to London and started fresh.'

'Well, Dad did. You know he married again a few years later?'

Roisin nodded.

'I blamed myself for a long time, thinking there must be something wrong with me, and that's why she never came back.'

'Oh, Glen.' Roisin's throat tightened. She couldn't fathom the hurt he must have felt.

'But as I got older, I realised it was her, not me. She was a drunk, Roisin. She loved the bottle more than her family. She had good spells, but the bad episodes began to take over until I never knew which Mam I'd find when I walked in the door from school. I'd have put up with that, though, if it meant she'd stayed.'

Roisin's vision was blurred as she blinked the tears away, and they came to a standstill on the stone bridge leading back to the village where she'd stood watching the water rush under it earlier. His words shocked Roisin. She'd had no clue Aunty Dara drank when they'd stayed. Glen reached into his pocket and withdrew a packet of cigarettes. His hand shook as he held it out to Roisin.

She shook her head. 'No, thanks.'

He tapped a cigarette out of the box. 'I don't smoke either. Or so I tell myself.' He patted down his pockets until he found his lighter. The rasp of the flint sounded, and he lit his cigarette, dragging on it deeply. 'What happened left its scars.' Glen uttered his words through a stream of smoke. 'I think that's what Suzie was trying to mend by inviting her here.'

Roisin didn't say anything. There was nothing she could say. It was better to listen, and they stood in silence with the water babbling beneath them. A flock of birds were black specks on the sky, which was slowly deepening to a rosy hue, and a mosquito whined somewhere near Roisin's ear. She batted it away, not wishing to be bitten on top of her earlier sting.

'What would you do?' Glen asked, dropping the smoke and grinding it out with his heel. He rested his hands on the stone wall.

'I don't know, Glen. I do know forgiveness is hard, though.' Colin's face floated before her. The lies he'd told her culminated in them losing their home. Had she forgiven him? It gave her a jolt to realise she had. All that anger had ebbed away without her even realising it. She'd gained nothing from allowing it to suck her energy.

What was it about this stream? she wondered. She knew the sound of water was good for meditation, which undoubtedly gave her clarity. So she decided that a water feature wherever she wound up living would be a good investment. That, or it would make her need the loo.

The risk of taking that next step with Shay and maybe being hurt again had made her wary, and she'd held a part of herself back from him. That wasn't living, though, and it came to her then that there was no point in holding onto past hurts because their only purpose was to limit your future. She told Glen this.

'You sound very wise and profound, Roisin.'

'It's because I do yoga,' she replied as though that explained everything.

She was rewarded with a grin. He nodded slowly. 'I've been thinking of taking it up to see if it helps me with my squash.'

'It will,' Roisin assured him. 'And you should. It's what oil is to car parts for your joints.'

They stood in silence once more until Roisin spoke up. 'Will you listen to what she's come to say? She's come a long way, and you're not that little boy anymore. You've already experienced the worst kind of hurt and survived it. She asked me to tell you she was sorry. So did Suzie.'

His grip tightened on the wall, then slowly relaxed. 'What you said before about accepting what you're told as a child made me think. I only ever heard my dad's version of why she left. I'd like to hear hers.'

Roisin nodded and threaded her arm through his. 'Come on then. Let's find her.'

They heard the strains of 'Maggie' drifting down the lane as they neared the house, and Roisin, to ease Glen's apprehension, shared her earlier prediction. 'What's the bet the lot of them will have their arms around each other's shoulder having a sing-a-long?' Even though the twilight was ebbing, she saw the ghost of a smile playing at the corners of Glen's mouth. He knew she was right, proved once they'd ducked down the side path to the garden.

The drink had been flowing in their absence, and the gathered O'Maras gave the Irish folk music duo's song their all. All that was missing were the karaoke screens and microphones. Nevertheless, their not-so-dulcet tones were a blessing because to do the great Foster & Allen justice was of far more importance than paying Glen and Roisin any heed. Besides, family drama was par for the course at any shindig, and the earlier to-do over the unexpected arrival of Dara O'Mara was swiftly forgotten as they'd returned to the business of reminiscing and singing.

Roisin scanned the garden but could see no sign of her sisters or Tom and Quinn, whom she presumed had taken their babies back to the hotel, escaping before the singing started.

Donal was sharing a joke with Geordie O'Mara, and Noah and his friend were waving sparklers about trying to write their names on the air. She'd no clue where they'd got them from, but they were having a whale of a time and, waving to her son, she saw he'd jam and cream smeared around his mouth.

'Would you like a piece of cake?' One of the youth club youngsters held a tray out under her nose. On it was squares of sponge cake filled with evidence of what Noah had been enjoying in her absence.

Roisin's mouth watered, but she said, 'No, you're grand, thanks.' There was no time to be standing about eating cake.

Glen declined too. The girl moved off, stopping to let Noah and his friend help themselves to a second or, for all Roisin knew, a third helping of the sponge. She predicted her son would crash and burn very soon. Thank goodness Poppa D was on hand to deal with that, she thought, remembering what they'd come to do.

'My guess is they'll either be inside' – she gestured to the house – 'or they'll have headed back to the hotel. Will we go and see?'

Glen held his hand out in an after-you gesture, happy to let Roisin take the lead as she ventured into the kitchen. Her eyes watered at the smell of onions chopped on the worktop that afternoon and, ignoring Uncle Bartley as he exited the bathroom still fiddling with his fly, she carried on through to the front room before he could offer her any cheese.

Mammy, Noreen, Suzie and Dara sat in the chintzy front room with a pot of tea on the coffee table between them. Framed photographs of the corner shop Great Aunt Noreen had run with her late husband decorated the walls, and an array of family photographs vied for space on the side cabinet. These were of a younger Emer and her siblings whom Roisin had met throughout the afternoon and evening.

The teacup rattled dangerously in its saucer as Dara put it down on the table, seeing Roisin appear in the doorway with Glen behind her. She stood up, smoothing her green dress and tucking back the wisps of hair that had fallen free from her bun. Suzie's gaze was anxious as she tried to read Glen's expression, but he wasn't giving anything away.

'Come and sit down,' Noreen urged, standing with a sprightliness belying her years.

Maureen drained her cup and joined her. Roisin looked to Glen. She'd done her part and brought him back. What happened next between him, Dara and Suzie was their business.

Glen sat on the edge of the sofa Noreen and Maureen had just vacated, looking as though he was poised to take flight.

'There's tea left in the pot if you fancy a cup, Glen. You'll find a cup and saucer in the kitchen. Come on, Maureen, we'll leave them to catch up, shall we? I fancy a slice of the cream cake the young ones should be passing around. Emer and I baked it. The Victoria sponge is my speciality, you know.'

'I'm hoping there's a piece with my name on it, Noreen,' Maureen whispered as the trio left the room, pulling the door behind them.

Chapter Twenty-five

'I'm sorry I didn't tell you Dara was coming, but I knew if I had—' Suzie, sitting with her hands clasped tightly, didn't finish her sentence.

Glen's face was unreadable, his mouth set in a firm line, and he wouldn't meet her gaze as he stared down at his shoes. But he'd come back. That counted for something, she thought, hearing the ticking of the carriage clock on the sideboard overly loud in the silence. She cleared her throat and opened her mouth to speak again but couldn't find the right words to say and looked instead to Dara, whose hands were also working on her lap as she stared at her son, drinking in the sight of him.

'Glen,' Dara said as though she simply wanted to say her son's name out loud. He didn't look up, and when she spoke, her voice threatened to break as she said in that jumbled accent, 'Oh my. You can't know how it feels to see you again.' Her eyes, mirrored versions of her son's, were overly bright. 'I've waited so long.'

This time Glen's head snapped up. 'It was you who left us. Not the other way around.'

'It wasn't by choice, Glen. I never wanted to leave you and your father.'

'But you did.'

'I didn't want to go, but your father made the right decision-making me leave. I wasn't a well woman, son.'

Glen bristled, holding his hand up and shaking his head. 'Don't call me that.'

'I'm sorry.' Dara bit her lip, and a tear tracked down her face.

'Glen, let her speak,' Suzie said softly, knowing if he would let Dara say her piece, it might help him understand what had happened all those years ago.

Glen looked at Suzie for the first time then, and the tense set of his shoulders softened a little after a moment. 'Go on.'

Suzie gave Dara a slight nod of encouragement. 'Tell him what you told me, Dara.'

'I-I wasn't looking after you the way a mammy should. The drink, you know. It came first. I don't know when it took over, but it did. My dad was the same. A Jekyll and Hyde. I vowed I'd never be like him, but it was in me, and I couldn't stop, not even after I hurt you.' She looked at his arm, but a shirt sleeve covered the puckered flesh.

Glen automatically pulled his scarred arm into himself protectively.

'I'll never forgive myself for that. Hugh couldn't forgive me either, and I don't blame him.' Dara was speaking quickly, as though frightened she'd not get the opportunity to finish what she'd come a long way to say. 'It was after that he contacted my sister, Marnie, who'd emigrated with her husband to Canada years earlier, and between the two of them it was decided the best thing for you would be if I came out to Canada. She'd found a clinic where I could go and get well. So, I went. I wanted to say goodbye to you, but Hugh thought that would only serve to upset you. He said he'd explain to you. I couldn't argue with him. Not after what I'd done.'

Glen's nod was curt.

'I wrote to you daily while in that clinic.'

'I never saw your letters.'

'I wondered.'

Suzie thought of Hugh receiving those early letters when his hurt and anger over not just an avoidable accident but years of secrecy and shame was still fresh. She wondered if Glen was thinking of them too.

'I did get better eventually, and I telephoned Hugh to say I'd like to come home. I didn't know if we could work things out, but I hoped we could for your sake.'

Roisin felt Glen tense at this.

'He didn't you tell that.' Dara's voice was resigned now.

'No.'

'I had no money for the fare home to Ireland, and my sister wasn't in a position to help me. Marnie and I weren't close, and she felt she'd done her bit. I'd made my bed, she'd say. So I found lodgings and a cleaning job, thinking if I could prove to Hugh that I was reliable enough to hold down a job, he'd decide I could be relied upon as a wife and mother again and give me a second chance. All the letters I sent to him at our old address were returned to sender and, in desperation, I wrote to Maureen. She told me Hugh had taken you to London, and she managed to find an address for me. I wrote to you both there, and your father replied this time.'

Dara paused, overcome, and Suzie, who could feel the weight of the past in the air she was breathing, took hold of her hand to help her find the strength to finish her story.

'Hugh told me it was a new life you were after making for yourselves.' Her voice shook. 'You were doing well, he told me, and had settled into your new school. For me to come back would undo all that. It wouldn't be fair. I was heartbroken, but the day I spilt that pan of boiling water on you because I was drunk was the day I felt I relinquished my rights to be your mother.'

'I thought it was my fault for years,' Glen said. 'I thought if I'd left you alone in the kitchen that evening to get on with it instead of hovering about trying to make sure you didn't hurt yourself, it wouldn't have happened, and you'd not have gone away.'

Tears were falling freely down Dara's cheeks now.

'Dad did what he thought was best for me.'

Dara gave a small nod. 'I know that.'

'It doesn't mean he did what was right, though,' Suzie said, getting up and moving to sit next to Glen. 'I wonder if your father kept those letters deliberately. He could have thrown them away,' she said, angling her body toward him and trying to take one of his hands in hers.

He pulled away, though and, bowing his head massaged his temples.

'Maybe he couldn't bring himself to tell you what had happened to your mam, but wanted you to know. He must have.'

Glen was silent mulling this over.

'It's a lot to take in and a shock to see me after so many years, I realise that,' Dara ventured.

'Why now? I mean, why did you come?'

'Suzie wrote to me and told me Hugh had passed. I wanted you to know that I'm here and never stopped loving you.'

'I don't know where we even begin to start.'

'Maybe from here. This moment right now.' Dara reached across, holding her hand out to Glen.

Suzie held her breath, willing him to take it, knowing she couldn't push any more than she already had.

Dara's hand didn't falter and, at last, Glen reached out and took it.

Chapter Twenty-six

'So, you'd no clue Dara was an alcoholic, Mammy? Or, why she really went to Canada?' Roisin asked as they picked their way back to the hotel under cover of the stars.

They'd only stayed at the party for another half hour, having given Noah a countdown. He'd been jabbing a sparkler like a light sabre at his friend, who, it turned out, was a second cousin twice removed, as they jousted, both boys happily ignoring Maureen's Magna Doodle message that they'd take an eye out doing that if they didn't watch it. Finally, thirty minutes later, the last of the sparklers were doused in a bucket of cold water, and they were off, with neither child requiring first aid. Now, Roisin leaned in close to hear Maureen's reply.

'No. Hugh never breathed a word about it to your daddy or me.' She sighed, sucking furiously on her Fisherman's Friend before carrying on in her weak voice. 'I suppose he was embarrassed. You're going back thirty years, Roisin. Times were different. Things weren't spoken about like they are now. I'll say this, though. It's a disservice he did Glen not telling him the truth about his poor mammy.'

Roisin made a noise of agreement. She thought so, too, knowing how the young Glen had perceived his mother's leaving.

'We don't always give our children enough credit, Roisin. We assume they won't cope with adult problems, but that's not always the case.'

'Maureen, you're supposed to be resting that voice,' Donal called back. He was a little ahead of them, with Noah piggybacking a ride.

Roisin thought her mammy very wise, and she linked her arm through hers as they strolled back to their accommodation.

They let themselves into the hotel. The foyer was empty and in shadows, given the only light was a lamp left on for guests returning after dark at the front desk. Roisin was tempted to check behind the drapes to make sure Angus or Herman, as she'd nicknamed him, wasn't lurking behind them waiting to spring out, but there was no sign of him. Then, taking to the stairs, they headed to their respective rooms. She was about to say goodnight to Noah when he pulled on his Poppa D's arm. Donal bent down to hear what he wanted to say, and Roisin waited, bemused, wondering what Noah was whispering about.

'I think that's an excellent idea, Noah.' Donal straightened then, looking to Roisin, added, 'Your son here's worried about you being on your own tonight, so he's decided he'll bunk in with you.' He winked over Noah's head, and Roisin gave a sage nod. 'I've told him his nana, and I will be alright without him.'

'That's very thoughtful of you, Noah, and I'll sleep a lot better having you in the room there with me, son.' He'd never been any different, Roisin mused as he said night-night to his grandparents. When he was worn out like he was now, he wanted her, and it was lovely, she thought, her heart melting a little as she determined to make the most of a snuggle with him because she knew it wouldn't always be the case.

She turned to wave night-night to her mammy, who blew her and Noah a kiss, then smiled as Donal called softly down the hall, 'Goodnight, John Boy!'

'Goodnight, John Boy!' she called back, knowing she'd have to explain the phrase to Noah before shutting the door and telling him they'd sort his things out in the morning. He could sleep in his shorts and tee shirt because, sure, what was a holiday if you couldn't do things differently?

'I can't brush my teeth either, Mummy, because my bags are in Nana and Poppa D's room.'

'Just this once, we'll let it go.' Roisin discarded her clothes, eager for her nighty, and after washing her face and brushing her teeth, clambered into bed next to her son, switching off the light.

Noah cuddled next to her, and his voice was muffled as he said, 'Good night, John Boy.'

She smiled, repeating it back to him. She could tell he had his thumb in his mouth. It was a habit Colin was determined to break. Granny Quealey had even painted that horrible-tasting stuff on his thumb, much to Roisin's annoyance, but he'd persevered and had grown sneaky about when he did it. Roisin didn't see the big deal. It was his thumb. He was only young, and if it gave him comfort, so be it.

She could smell smoke clinging to his hair from the BBQ as she stroked his head gently, listening to his breathing as it grew slow and steady, signalling he was asleep, leaving her alone with her thoughts, which turned to Glen.

What a burden he'd carried with him all these years. It was so easy to damage a child unwittingly. Adults blithely went about doing what they thought was best for themselves and their children, unaware of their actions' effects. How would Noah process Colin's news when they returned to London? she wondered. It was up to her and Colin to ensure he didn't harbour confusion over why his daddy was moving to Dubai. She made a silent promise to Noah, feeling his warmth burrowed into her, that she would always be open and honest with him to the best of her ability.

The mattress springs were digging into her sides, and she shifted, trying to get comfortable. That Noah would have to adapt to moving to Ireland, which would mean a new school and making new friends, churned away at her. The quiet was unnerving, she thought, unused to it. There was no steady thrum of traffic, the rumble of trains or wailing sirens and the deep belly-breathing wasn't helping her drift off. Instead, it merely sounded loud to her ears.

Noah mumbled something in his sleep, and she gave up. Was moving back home to Ireland the best thing for them? It was a relief to find that the answer from whichever angle she looked at it was the same each time. Yes.

Then having exhausted that line of thought, she pondered what had been said between Glen and Dara in Great Aunt Noreen's living room. She hoped Glen understood Suzie's intentions were good where his mother was concerned and that the outcome of having faced one another after so many years would give them a modicum of peace at least.

Mammy drove them all potty a lot of the time, but she was their rock. No matter what life threw their way, she was there for each of her children to pick up the pieces and spur them on. Roisin knew only some had that. They were lucky.

A stealthy creak of protesting floorboards beneath that well-worn carpet sounded in the corridor outside her room, and her eyes rounded wide in the dark, listening out. Common sense told her it was a straggler from the barbeque who'd probably fallen asleep in the hedgerow on the way home, having woken up once the night air had begun to turn chilly. Her imagination, however, pictured Herman Munster patrolling the floors of the hotel, but hearing Maggie being hummed saw her relax once more or at least as much as she could when trying her hardest to get off to sleep.

It was Shay's turn to step onto the conveyer belt of her thoughts next. How would she word what she wanted to say to him? She whispered various versions up at the ceiling, and then finally, just as the birds began to chirp, Roisin drifted off.

Chapter Twenty-seven

Roisin woke with a jolt, unsure what it was that had roused her until she felt the bed bouncing and, opening a gritty eye, saw Noah pretending he was on a trampoline next to her.

'Knock on Nana and Poppa D's door,' she croaked. 'Tell Nana your mammy says you need to brush your teeth, have a wash and put on some clean clothes. And don't be bouncing on the bed like so.'

Noah scampered off, and she heard the door bang shut behind him. The room was fully light thanks to the wafer-thin curtains, and sounds of life were reverberating through the hotel, but it wasn't yet eight, she saw with a glance at the clock on the set of drawers beside the bed. Whatever happened to having a lie-in on your holidays? It was probably on account of the breakfast. Nobody wanted to miss out. She could hear water running through the adjoining wall, and tossing the covers aside decided a shower would sort her out.

As it happened, a tepid trickle had to suffice.

Roisin took her time getting ready. Despite the lukewarm shower, which had done little to blast away the cobwebs, once she'd faffed with her hair, dabbed some concealer under her eyes to hide the dark circles, added a sweep of mascara and lipstick, she felt ready to join the human race. Especially given her lips were now nearly back to their normal size.

Today, she'd slipped into a whimsical dress with a rosy pink print she knew Shay liked, not caring if Mammy gave out about her not wearing the tee shirt and Mo-pants. A tee shirt with O'Mara Reunion 2002 on it was not what you wanted to wear when you told the man you loved you wanted to move back to Dublin and would like it if he'd move in with you and start trying for a baby all in one go. No, today was a whimsical dress day because somewhere between the hours of three and four am, she'd decided today she'd take a leaf out of Dara's book and be brave. She'd say her piece when Shay arrived later this morning.

First things first, though, and stepping out into the corridor and waving a greeting at Aunty Maeve, who was calling Uncle Paudie a heathen as she tucked the back of his shirt into his trousers outside their room, she needed a coffee.

The dining room was abuzz with chatter and the scrape of cutlery. Roisin stood in the doorway, looking to see if she was the first to make it downstairs. It took her less than a second to spy Mammy holding the Magna Doodle aloft with the words 'We're over here' printed on it. Donal, Noah, Moira, Tom and Kiera in a highchair were all seated around the table, tucking into their continental breakfasts. There was no sign of Aisling, Quinn and the twins as yet and, holding her hand up in acknowledgement, Roisin left Mammy to get back to her cereal and headed toward the table where the breakfast things were set out.

Uncle Geordie was already there, bowl in hand, debating between the cereal choices of All Bran flakes, Cocoa Pops or good old cornflakes.

'Have the bran, Geordie,' his wife, Cliona, looked over her shoulder from where she was pouring hot water onto her tea bag. Then seeing Roisin standing alongside her husband added. 'He takes forever on the throne of a morning. Nobody else gets a look in. Nor do they want to by the time he's finished. The bran will do him good, so it will. Tell him, Roisin. It gets things moving.'

Then she moved off with her tea and a plate of toast, leaving Roisin bewildered as to why her aunt thought she held any sway with Uncle Geordie when it came to his breakfast choices or, for that matter, why she was in the know when it came to the benefits of bran for breakfast.

Nevertheless, she was starving and wanted to get this show on the road. 'Sure, it's very good for you the bran, Uncle Geordie,' she said. Then added for good measure, 'Very good indeed.'

Gratifyingly, Geordie made up his mind and pulled the dispenser lever receiving a miserly serving of brown flakes. 'Sure, that wouldn't rev up a mouse's bowel,' he said, staring at the contents of his bowl. 'And where's the sultanas? Look it, can you see any?' He shook the bowl at Roisin before poking a finger amidst the flakes to check none were hiding.

'There aren't any, Uncle Geordie. They're All Bran flakes by the looks of that.'

Geordie snorted. 'All Bran flakes my arse. Greed is what that is, Roisin. Tight-fisted cereal company trying to save money by getting rid of the sultanas.'

Christ on a bike. All she wanted was a cup of coffee and a bowl of cornflakes. Surely it wasn't too much to ask? Roisin gulped down a calming breath. There was no point in getting all red in the face like

Uncle Geordie was. It wouldn't do any good. 'Why don't you add some cornflakes to them? Jazz it up a little?' she suggested.

Geordie looked at her like she was daft but then thought twice about it and pointed to the Cocoa Pops container. 'What are those there?'

'Cocoa Pops, Uncle Geordie. They're chocolatey. You'll like those. They'll sweeten up your bran flakes.' Jaysus wept. What was with all the rodent remarks? she thought as he mumbled they looked like giant mouse poo before jostling her out of the way so he could hold his bowl under the canister. 'Sure, Cliona's blind as a bat. She'll think they're the sultanas and stop giving out to me about the bran,' he added, pulling the lever.

Nothing happened.

Roisin ran through her repertoire of religious sayings deciding this was a Holy God Above Tonight moment as Uncle Geordie rattled the lever back and forth as though his life depended on it.

She could have kissed Noah when he popped up beside them and said, 'There's a trick to the Cocoa Pops. Let me show you.'

Geordie released the lever, and Noah, as though cracking a safe code, tweaked it up then down, gave it a little shake and one last tweak up. It was like magic seeing a tumble of Cocoa Pops shoot down into Geordie's bowl.

There were pats on the back for Noah and a cash donation for his troubles of five pence. Roisin thought it was on the nose, given less than two minutes earlier he'd been banging on about the mercenary cereal companies. What was a lad supposed to buy with five pence? Noah, however, was delighted, and Geordie was delighted, and in the end, so was Roisin as they both moved away, leaving her to fetch her cornflakes and pour a much-needed cup of coffee.

She carried her cornflakes over to the thermos marked coffee, seeing there was a toaster with bread in a basket and a pair of tongs alongside it. A selection of spreads in those little pots with the peel-off lid was in a lucky-dip bowl. She'd come back for toast, she decided, and maybe she'd have one of those speckly bananas in the bowl there and a scone for afters, too. Then again, she thought, giving the scones a second glance, maybe not. They looked like they could be lobbed as weapons. She poured her coffee and was about to add milk to her cereal and steaming brew but saw the jug was empty. That was when Herman Munster emerged from the curtain behind the table, and she nearly tipped the hot brown liquid all over herself in fright.

Herman grunted something unintelligible and whisked the jug off for a refill.

Like a bad smell, Uncle Bartley materialised by her side, waiting until Herman had disappeared through the door to the kitchen to help himself to a heap of the sugar sachets. No wonder he was missing so many teeth, Roisin thought as he gave her a grin as chequered as his trousers. The same pair he'd had on yesterday, she noticed, shuddering. And how he managed to slide a finger in their pocket, let alone squash all those packets of sugar into trousers so tight, was a mystery worthy of Sherlock Holmes himself.

She frowned hard, willing him to get on his way. But the Gods, it would seem, were not shining down on her this morning.

'He watches yer like a hawk, that one.' Bartley nodded toward the door, which Herman had just disappeared through. 'Told me off he did for taking too many sugars for my tea. Can I help it if I have a sweet tooth when it comes to my tea?' He eyed her up and down. 'It's Roisin, isn't it? Maureen's oldest girl.'

For a moment, Roisin was tempted to pretend she was a Russian tourist called Olga, but against her better judgement, she nodded.

'Well now, Roisin, I've some cheese back at my table that spreads like butter on the toast. It's lovely, so it is. Would you care to join me?'

Roisin risked a glance at him in time to receive a leery wink, and channelling Moira, she smiled sweetly and said, 'I can't, Uncle Bartley. I'm lactose intolerant. Dairy products, cheese, in particular, gives me terrible diarrhoea.'

Uncle Bartley looked past her then to the door leading to the kitchen and, seeing Herman push through it, to Roisin's relief, scuttled off.

The milk jug was placed in front of her in silence, and she saw Herman eyeing the contents of her cereal bowl as she poured milk over the cornflakes. She was glad she'd not gone for that third lever pull. When she next looked up, he'd melted back into the curtains, and after stirring her coffee, she carried her breakfast over to the table where her family was gathered and slotted in alongside Moira.

'Good morning, all. Jaysus, what an ordeal that was.'

'Tell me about it,' Moira said. 'I saw Uncle Bartley offered you the cheese. What did you say to get him moving off at the speed of light like so?'

Roisin relayed what she'd said, and Moira laughed.

'I can't take full credit. I think he was worried Herman lurking in the curtains over there would make him put the sugar back if he copped on to all the sachets he'd helped himself to. What's he doing having breakfast here anyway? I thought he was staying at Great Aunt Noreen's?'

'Apparently, she's a full house, with Freya and her brother and sister staying. So she sent him back here to the hotel.'

'But he never pays for accommodation.'

'He's not. He slept in his car.'

Both sisters pulled a face before Moira got back to spooning up her cornflakes, leaving Roisin to scan the room.

'No Glen or Suzie?' she asked, looking toward Maureen.

Maureen shook her head, and her frown told Roisin she was as desperate to know how things had panned out too. She ignored the Magna Doodle, sounding almost normal once again. 'No, I've not seen them nor Dara.' The frown deepened. 'Why're you not wearing your shirt?'

'I got tomato sauce down the front of it last night, Mammy.'

'I have a spare one in case of emergencies. Shall we go up and you can change into it?'

'No. You're grand. Sit and enjoy your breakfast.'

Roisin was grateful when Donal distracted her from pushing the point by getting up from the table. He laid a paw on Maureen's shoulder.

'I'm heading up for some toast. Can I get you a slice, Mo?' Donal said in an exceptionally cheery voice. 'It's a hearty appetite I'm after building up this morning.'

Maureen tittered. 'I'm famished myself. That would be lovely, Donal.'

'I'll have some of what they're having,' Roisin said to anyone who was listening, needing an injection of cheeriness.

'Not much chance of that until Shay gets here,' Moira replied tartly. 'And I'm not surprised that pair have worked up an appetite.'

Before Roisin could ask what she meant, however, she caught sight of Noah draining the milk from his cereal bowl by raising it to his mouth in a manner which would have her and her sisters clipped around the ear when they were younger. She fixed him with a hard stare, which he pretended not to notice, and then, putting the bowl down, made a satisfied 'aah' sound as though supping a pint. A ring of chocolate from the Cocoa Pops decorated his mouth. She doubted she'd ever look at the cereal the same again after her conversation with Uncle Geordie.

Tom was wrestling with Kiera for the spoon, which she was determined to splash in her bowl, while Moira spooned up the last of her cereal before pushing her bowl away.

'Will you be having toast, Moira? It's included in the price,' Maureen asked, seeing she'd finished. Then she gave Noah a nudge. 'Poppa D will help you put some on Noah.'

The little boy raced after Donal.

'You're sounding much better today, Mammy,' Roisin said.

''Tis the Fisherman's Friends I've to thank for that.'

Roisin could see the Fisherman's Friends were going to be to the throat what the E45 cream was to the skin.

'I will be,' Tom was quick to reply.

'Will be what?' Maureen had forgotten what she'd asked Moira a few seconds ago.

'Having toast.'

'Good. We'll be wanting our money's worth while we're here. It's inclusive, you know. Moira?' Maureen pointed to her empty bowl.

'Not for me. I'm not very hungry this morning, Mammy.' She pursed her lips primly, and the look she shot her mammy disapproving.

'Why are you glaring at me like so? What is it I'm supposed to have done?'

'Cast your mind back, Mammy, to first thing this morning.'

'Tom, will you tell the mother of your babby there I've no clue what she's on about.' Maureen shook her head, sending her hair swishing back and forth.

Tom had gone mottled shades of red, Roisin noticed, shovelling in her cornflakes, wondering what Mammy was after doing that had Moira in a tizz and Tom blushing.

'I'm not saying it out loud in the presence of children,' Moira stated prudishly.

'For every problem, there's a solution Moira.' Maureen passed the Magna Doodle over the table, adding through gritted teeth, 'Spell it out.'

Moira held up two fingers.

'Don't be doing the rude-finger sign at me, young lady.'

'I'm not. It's two words.' Moira dipped her dark head and wrote on the board before showing it to Mammy, whose mouth formed an 'O'.

'Let me see,' Roisin demanded.

Moira spun the board round, and Roisin read, 'Headboard Banging'.

'What does that mean?' There was a mental clunk as the penny dropped. Could her morning get any worse? Mammy and Donal? NO! It didn't bear thinking about it. Surely not at their age. It wasn't right.

Moira correctly read the myriad expressions flitting across her big sister's face as she processed what she'd just learned. 'My thoughts exactly.'

Maureen recovered and donned a cat that got the cream sort of smile. 'I've said it before, and I'll say it again. You young wans think you invented the bedroom shenanigans, so you do.'

'What's going on?' Aisling asked. Kieran was strapped to her chest.

Tom, Roisin saw was checking out the breakfast offerings.

'Don't ask!' Moira and Roisin chimed.

Chapter Twenty-eight

♥

'Tom and I thought we'd go for a run, seeing as the weather's turned it on for us again. It's like being in the south of France on your holidays,' Quinn announced as the group filed out of the dining room, coming to a halt in the reception lounge to discuss their plans for the day ahead. He was yet to change into his running gear but was already warming up with his foot in his hand, bending his leg behind him.

It was a stretch to compare the south of France to Claredoncally, Roisin thought, amused. Where was the sea, for one thing? It did look like another glorious day was waiting to greet them, though, so there'd be no complaints from her.

Her phone, which she'd been checking every five minutes since she got up waiting to hear from Shay, finally beeped. 'He's on his way!' she looked up from his text message receiving indulgent smiles of acknowledgement.

'Absence makes the heart grow fonder,' Aisling said with a smile at her sister.

'Does he run, Roisin?' Tom didn't pause in his lunging.

He was putting Roisin in mind of Mammy demonstrating her Mo-pants, although she'd not been so gung-ho to do so of late, given the pain in her knee. 'Sometimes.'

'Maybe we can talk him into coming for an early-morning jog tomorrow before we get on the road. It'll make a nice change to breathe in the country air instead of exhaust fumes,' Tom said, then looked to Donal. 'You're welcome to join us, Donal, given how sprightly you feel this morning.' There was a definite smirk on Tom's face.

'And, if your knees are up to it,' Quinn added, his blue eyes dancing.

Aisling elbowed her husband. 'Behave!'

Donal was oblivious to the in-joke, but Maureen wiped the smiles off both her son-in-laws' faces with a fierce stare from one to the other.

'No. Sure lads. I'd only slow you down. Sadly, my running days are over,' he replied.

'Not your riding days, though.'

'What was that Moira?' Donal asked.

'Nothing.' She busied herself, wiping Kiera's nose before she wiped it on her daddy's shoulder.

'A stroll with Mo here's what the doctor ordered. So you lads, enjoy yourselves.'

'You want to watch out for the tractors,' Maureen warned. 'And the magpies. Terrible, vicious they are swooping and pecking like so. You'll be beacons to them, the pair of you in that bright running gear you're so fond of wearing.'

'That's only in spring when they're protecting their babbies, Mammy,' Aisling contradicted. 'You can hardly blame them.'

'If we can deal with the Dublin pigeons, we can handle a magpie or two.' Tom laughed, recounting how a manky bird had reared up, flapping away at himself and Quinn when they were putting themselves through the paces alongside the canal the other day. They'd put on a holy show warding the thing off. 'It was like a scene from that Hitchcock film, *The Birds*,' he finished.

'It would be nice to show Kiera some cows or a sheep while we're here,' Moira said, and there was much nodding and agreement that yes, it would be nice.

An exploratory walk around the village lanes, followed by morning tea in the village tea rooms was agreed upon. Maureen told them she was keen to test out her new walking shoes purchased from Carrick's the Cobblers in Howth.

'But what about the tractors and magpies?' Moira asked.

'Sure, we'll be grand. It's not us who'll be dressed like a couple of jogging peacocks,' Maureen dismissed the comment, eager to get the show on the road.

Roisin decided it was better not to say that the lads' bright running gear would help the farmer on the tractor see them, or they'd never get out the door. Not that she planned on joining them. 'I'm going to wait for Shay.'

'Ah no, Roisin, come with us. Sure, he'll find you.' Maureen tutted. ''Tis a village we're after walking about, not New York City.'

'But I want to be here when he arrives, Mammy. You know, to greet him. He's gone to a lot of effort to get here.'

'I want to see Shay too. I'll stay here with Mummy.' Noah moved to Roisin's side.

Maureen gave Roisin the 'now look what you've done' face.

Roisin shrugged. She didn't mind if Noah wanted to hang about here with her. It was lovely he wanted to be here when Shay arrived.

'Leave a note with Deirdre over there to say we've gone for a walk, and Shay can join us,' Maureen fluttered her hands in Deirdre's direction, receiving a scowl. 'The fresh air will put roses in Noah's cheeks, so it will, and a little birdy's after telling me there's ice cream to be found at the Spar up the road there.'

'It was a magpie who told you that, was it?' Moira asked tongue in cheek.

'Nana, did the little birdy tell you if they had those Iceberger ones you always buy me when I come to see you?'

'It did, Noah.'

Noah moved to stand next to his Nana.

He was easily bought her son, Roisin thought, still pleading her case. 'Shay might not want to go for a walk, Mammy. It's Germany he's after flying in from. He might be tired and need a lie-down.' She was beginning to wish Mammy hadn't got her voice back.

Moira snorted, hearing this.

'Mammy, Kieran's going to kick off if we don't get the pram moving,' Aisling said, rocking it back and forth.

'But what will you do with yourself while you're waiting?' Maureen asked, weakening.

'I've a book I've been trying to finish for ages. So I'll sit over there in the sun and read it. I'll be grand.'

Satisfied, Maureen gave the nod, leaving Quinn and Tom to go and change into their running gear. Then, the rest of the family headed out the door.

Roisin retrieved her murder mystery book from her room and returned to the sofa. Her back was to the trickle of O'Maras venturing out and about, leaving her in peace to read. There was no sign of Herman hiding behind the drapes, but she could feel Deirdre's beady eyes boring into her back now and again as she skimmed over the text, eager to find out who did it. She thought she had it all figured out but suspected a twist might be coming, mainly because it said there was a twist you wouldn't see coming on the cover.

AN O'MARA'S REUNION

The story had her gripped, and she didn't notice the presence alongside where she was sitting until she heard Suzie's voice.

'I thought it was you hiding away over here. Morning, Roisin. Good book?'

'Morning.' Roisin smiled back, thinking Suzie looked tired, which she supposed was to be expected after the events of the night before. She put her bookmark in place and snapped the novel shut. 'It's a proper whodunnit.' She looked past Suzie and, seeing no sign of Glen or Dara – if she was still there – patted the seat next to her in invitation. 'Join me.'

'Are you sure? I don't want to drag you away from your book.'

'Don't be silly.'

'Thanks, then I will. Glen and Dara are just finishing breakfast,' she explained, flopping beside her. Today, Suzie was dressed in practical travel gear and looked ready for a day's exploring. She had a *Rough Guide to Ireland* in her hand, and a pair of sunglasses pushed up onto her head. 'It was quite a night,' she said, stifling a yawn.

The yawn was contagious, and Roisin apologised. 'Sorry! And you're right. It was. I've been thinking about you all.'

Suzie's smile was rueful. 'Thirty years is a long time.'

'It is.'

'Glen and Dara had a lot of ground to cover.'

Roisin nodded but didn't say anything, hoping the years hadn't left a hole between them too big to traverse.

Suzie's eyes, however, were shining. 'Glen listened though, and he talked. They even hugged.'

'Ah, Suzie, that's great.'

She nodded. 'It's a start.'

'A good start,' Roisin affirmed.

'Yeah, it is.' They smiled at one another. 'Dara didn't stay away all these years by choice,' Suzie said, gripping the guidebook as she relayed the sad story to Roisin.

By the time she'd finished, Roisin was rummaging in her bag for a tissue. It was sad, but she firmly believed in second chances and new beginnings, and hoped Glen and Dara would now have theirs. Locating the tissue, she dabbed her eyes and gave her nose a blow.

Suzie reached out and patted her knee. 'I think their story will have a happy ending.'

Roisin spying a rubbish bin, got up and dropped the sodden tissue into it, then sitting back down, said, 'I hope so.'

'Me too.' Suzie slapped her thighs, changing the subject. 'Anyway, what are your plans for today? We're going for a drive. There's a castle I don't want to miss, and we thought we'd have lunch in the town nearby.' She pointed to the guidebook on her lap. 'I forgot what it's called. Kin something or other. You're welcome to join us.'

'Thanks, but I'm waiting for my—' She never knew what to call him. 'Shay. He's a creative producer, which involves coordinating music festivals, and he's flown in from Germany this morning. He should be here soon.'

'Wow, that must be an interesting job.'

'He loves it.'

'What about you, Roisin? What do you do?'

Roisin chatted about her job and yoga and would have filled her in on the decisions she'd made yesterday, eager to confide in her, but Glen and Dara were exiting the dining room, and Suzie was already half out of her seat.

Roisin waved over, receiving one in return. She thought there'd be time to catch up with Glen later, then was surprised by Suzie suddenly grasping her hand.

AN O'MARA'S REUNION

'Thanks, Roisin, for bringing Glen back last night.'

'I only listened to him, that's all. He wanted to come back.' She squeezed Suzie's hand in return, and the American woman released it, heading over to join the waiting pair.

Roisin called out to them all to enjoy their day and watched them exit the hotel. She liked to think Suzie was right and that Glen and Dara would feature in one another's lives from here on. At the very least, Glen knew the truth about what had happened now. She shook her head, still struggling to grasp how Uncle Hugh, who'd always been an affable man, had wiped his ex-wife from their lives. The past was the past, though. It couldn't be changed, but the future could. Then, opening her book again, Roisin lost herself in the story. She'd flicked the page to the last chapter when a hand clasping her shoulder made her jump. She nearly dropped her book.

'Sorry, I didn't mean to startle you.'

Roisin twisted around to see Shay backlit, his fiddle case in one hand and a bag slung over his other shoulder. He travelled light, she thought, drinking him in. His preference for battered old jeans, black tee shirts and cowboy-styled boots meant you'd never know he was Irish. He looked like he'd be much more at home wandering up the dusty drive of a Montana ranch than standing here in Isaac's Hotel, Claredoncally. Snapping out of her trance, she shot out of her seat to welcome him. A hug was swiftly followed by a hungry kiss that had Deirdre making rumblings about clean establishments.

Roisin's tender lip felt bruised but she didn't mind in the slightest as they broke apart, smiling into one another's eyes.

'Where is everyone?' Shay asked.

'Out for a walk. It's just you and me. C'mon.' She led him by the hand to the stairs with a naughty wink that had Deirdre spluttering.

Chapter Twenty-nine

♥

Roisin and Shay emerged from the room, having decided to head out to find the others. Roisin's hair was still damp from the shower as they trooped back down the stairs. Shay was itching to see Noah, so to hurry things along, she'd not bothered blow-drying it and hoped it didn't frizz too much. She'd wondered whether Shay might need a nap because she knew his work involved burning the candle at both ends, and he'd flown from Berlin to Dublin to Cork before picking up a hire car and driving here. He was used to it, though, he said, insisting he was fine.

As they reached the foyer area, Roisin wondered when she'd find the right moment for the conversation she was determined they had. There'd been a window back in the room when she'd toyed with blurting it all out. He'd been propped up on one elbow gazing down at her, and it had been right there on the tip of her tongue, but before she could formulate a coherent sentence, a vacuum cleaner began whining outside their door. The moment vanished as Shay rolled onto his back and said he could do with a hot shower.

'Good luck with that,' she'd said, telling him the water had been lukewarm at best earlier then, getting up, she fetched the tee shirt Mammy had brought for him. She tossed it over to him, and he held it out in front of him, a little perplexed reading the logo.

'Mammy wants you to feel part of the family,' Roisin explained. 'It's a good thing.' She smiled, hoping he saw it that way, especially after meeting the extended O'Mara clan. Uncle Bartley, in particular, sprang to mind.

He'd hopped off the bed with a grin. 'Then I'll wear it with pride. An honorary O'Mara. Joining me?' He waggled his eyebrows.

'Well, we do have to conserve what little hot water there is.' Roisin trotted in after him happily.

Now, as they stepped outside the hotel onto the street, blinking in the bright sunshine like moles emerging from their tunnels, Roisin warned, 'Don't be making eye contact with any of the villagers.' She gave him the rundown of her encounters with the locals the previous day, making Shay laugh. Then taking her hand in his, they set off down the main street with no particular destination in mind, just enjoying being in one another's company. They made it to the stone bridge near the rectory without incident to see a familiar group ambling down the lane toward them. Mammy was waving out vigorously, and Noah broke ranks to come charging straight for Shay.

Roisin laughed as her son smacked into him, wrapping his arms around his legs and then screeching in delight as Shay picked him up and helicoptered him about.

'We're going to get ice cream! Nana's getting me an Iceberger,' he shouted. 'They're my favourites.'

'An Iceberger, you say? Well, I'm always up for an ice cream biscuit sandwich, so I am.'

Roisin's heart swelled, looking at them both, and she grinned inanely. It would all work out grand.

Shay was greeted warmly by the rest of the family, scoring brownie points with Maureen for wearing the tee shirt. Next, he fussed over the babies, unaware of how closely Roisin was watching him interact with them. Then they trooped back from where they'd come in search of the promised ice cream.

'We found a swimming hole by a field with three goats in it,' Noah told his mammy and Shay. 'Poppa D told me the Billy Goats Gruff story, and Nana says we're going to buy some ham and bread and lemonade to take back there for a picnic lunch and that I can have a swim. We're going to have ice cream first, then go back to the hotel to get Uncle Tom and Uncle Quinn, and we'll pick up the lunch things on our way out again.'

'Nana's got her voice back alright by the sounds of things,' Roisin said, laughing.

Moira piped up behind them. 'I didn't like how that brown goat looked at me, and you couldn't pay me to go for a dip. I stuck a toe in the water, and I'm telling you, Rosi, you'd freeze your—'

'Yes, that's enough thanks very much, Moira. We get the idea. You'd do well to remember there are young impressionable minds present.' Maureen's voice, gaining strength by the hour, wafted toward them.

It did sound like a nice idea, though, Roisin thought. Not the swimming in an arctic pond but a few hours lazing about on the grass listening to the bird song while nibbling at ham sandwiches, which would make a nice change from yesterday's egg. She could suggest she and Shay go for a walk while the others kept an eye on Noah. Talk then. She decided it was as good a plan as any, thinking she wouldn't mind a Cornetto herself.

AN O'MARA'S REUNION

Donal, Tom, Quinn and Shay were bent over, carting the picnic accessories as they trooped down the lane with Mammy at the helm. Roisin had pulled her aside as they'd sat on the wall outside the Spar enjoying their ice creams and told her what Suzie had said earlier. Maureen was as warmed by what seemed to be a happy outcome as Roisin was. Although she confided in Roisin she was still struggling to understand how the Hugh she and Brian knew could have completely cut his ex-wife out of their son's life. It was a question that would never be answered and one they supposed there was no point dwelling on.

So much for keeping the picnic simple with sandwiches and pop, Roisin mused. By the time they'd exited the convenience store, they had a choice of two salads, coleslaw and a dodgy mixed bean salad reduced to clear. That didn't bode well, in Roisin's opinion. She'd be steering clear, but Mammy couldn't resist a bargain. There was a loaf of white bread and wholemeal, with ham or turkey for the sandwich fillings. An argument had ensued over whether they could do without the buttery spread, which would melt in the warm weather and a vote was held with the spread being a necessity coming in four to two. Chocolate digestive biscuits and Tim Tams had been slipped into the shopping basket by an unknown source, along with a caramel shortcake on special. And, when it came to beverages, there'd been no skimping with orange, apple and tomato juice on offer, or fizzy orange and a bottle of lemonade for those who preferred bubbles in their drink, namely Noah.

'Are we nearly there?' Moira griped, scuffing her feet as they rounded yet another bend and saw nothing ahead but the same view of blue sky, fluffy clouds, fields and lane as the one they'd just left behind.

The sun, high in the sky, beat down on them all. The twins' pram had a sun shade covering them while Kiera perched up in her pushchair was slathered in sunscreen, shaded by a yellow sunhat covered in white daisies.

'Moira, you were with us when we found it. You know where it was as well as I do,' Maureen said with a touch of tetchiness due to the heat.

'At this rate, we'll all get fecking sunstroke,' Aisling griped, fanning herself as she tried to keep pace with Quinn. 'And my thighs are rubbing. I'm five steps away from the chaffing, so I am.'

'I told you to put a hat on,' Quinn admonished, glancing over at her pink face.

'But then I'd have hat hair at the dinner tonight.'

Roisin smiled up at Shay, who was listening to the banter around him with a grin. He was an only child, and she wondered what it was like for him to be thrown amid her mad lot like so, but he seemed to take it all in his stride.

'Listen,' Donal said, coming to a standstill and tilting his head to the left.

Ears were dutifully cocked to hear bleating in the distance. It was coming from the other side of the hedgerow.

'The Billy Goats Gruff!' Noah shouted, then running ahead for a few yards, he disappeared through an opening in the tangled greenery into the field beyond. The others, now with a spring in their step, given they were at their destination, followed suit.

'Doesn't it make you want to open your arms and start singing about the hills being alive?' Aisling said, forgetting all about being hot and bothered as she surveyed the vista.

'It does,' Roisin agreed, gazing about the grassy meadow covered in dancing daisies and red clover. One tree punctuated the view, which would provide shade for the perfect picnic spot. She thought all that was missing was a bridge over the river, spying the three goats, two white, one brown, grazing a short distance from the rushing water.

The river wasn't exactly the Liffey, and it must dwindle to a stream by the time it reached the stone bridge on the edge of the village, Roisin thought. As for the swimming hole, well, that was a loose term. A paddling pool would be a more accurate description. Still, Noah would enjoy getting wet and splashing about. The goats, she realised, had paused briefly and were eyeing the intruders in their meadow, but then deciding they weren't all that interesting, they got back to the lawn-mowing business.

'I don't trust those goats,' Moira muttered.

'Don't be silly, Moira. Sure, they barely looked up. They're not interested in us at all,' Maureen said then, looking to Kiera, whose pudgy arm was outstretched as she shouted something unintelligible at the goats, added, 'Sure, take a leaf out of your daughter's book there. She'd be riding them about the place bareback given half a chance.'

Moira looked unconvinced, keeping a wary eye on the goats as the picnic rug was unfurled and the feast unloaded.

Shay wandered down to the river edge to keep an eye on Noah, who'd pulled off his tee shirt, discarding it on the bank before plunging in and lying flat on his belly in the shallow pool. Quinn decided to let Kiera get her feet wet, too, and the rest of them arranged themselves on the rug and the grass under their leafy canopy watching the spectacle.

'This is what it's all about, Mo,' Donal said happily.

'It is Donal,' Maureen replied, passing him a paper plate she'd filled with a sandwich and salad. 'Apple or orange juice?'

'Apple, please.'

Roisin had to admit to feeling content as she listened to Kiera and Noah's squeals of delight. Shay was laughing at whatever the kids were doing, and Aisling gave her a nudge.

'He's a keeper, Rosi.'

Moira, overhearing, paused in dolloping coleslaw on her paper plate. 'Ash's right.'

'What are you three whispering about over there,' Maureen asked.

'Nothing, Mammy,' Roisin quickly replied before making up a plate for Noah. She knew full well that if she didn't, he'd put nothing but Tim Tams, chocolate-covered digestives and a slice of caramel shortcake on it. Her sisters weren't telling her anything she didn't already know.

Shay Redmond was a keeper.

Chapter Thirty

'Did Roisin tell she was after getting stung by a bee, right there?' Moira pointed to her lip and gave Shay a graphic description of what she'd looked like and how it was fortunate it had gone down overnight; otherwise, he might have been hopping on the plane back to Germany.

Shay was laughing at the visual she painted from where he was stretched out next to Roisin, who plucked a handful of grass and tossed it at her sister.

Noah was helping Kiera build a tower with stones he'd collected from the river bed, and the twins had been fed, changed and were enjoying a kick in the fresh air, fascinated by the leaves overhead. The picnic was a distant memory, and it had been agreed that the goats could have the remains of the bean salad, which only Maureen had been game to eat and the last of the digestives, which had melted and gone soft. There were a few rounds of bread up for donation, too, but right then, nobody could be bothered getting up. The leftovers could wait.

'Tell us about Germany, Shay,' Moira said. 'Who'd you meet this time around?'

His story about a popular DJ's demands that his favoured brand of toilet paper be located, or he'd not perform his mix, had them rolling about the place, and Roisin felt immensely proud of him. He fitted in so easily with them all. Sure, hadn't she even heard him agree to join Quinn and Tom on their early-morning run tomorrow? More fool him.

'We should think about getting back to the hotel. There are drinks in the bar before dinner,' Maureen said from where she was leaning against Donal. 'Moira, I think you should take the scraps down to the goats.'

'And why would I want to do that?'

'Because the best way to overcome your fears is to face them head-on.'

'Mammy, I don't have a fear of goats. I don't like the brown one, is all. He was looking at me funny earlier.'

'Sure, he was not. You think everybody's always after looking at you funny.'

Moira, seeing Mammy take a deep breath about to launch into a story, put the kibosh on it. 'I will feed the goats on the condition you don't start telling the story of how when strangers came up to me as a baby to tell you what a beautiful babby I was I'd scream the place down.'

Maureen mimed, zipping her lips shut as Moira scrambled to her feet and, gathering up the leftovers, marched through the grass to the goats. 'See,' she called back with a swish of dark hair, 'not frightened.'

'I'm going to take a photograph,' Maureen said. 'Donal, would you help me up.'

Donal obliged and, camera in hand, Maureen trotted after her daughter. The others all sat up to watch.

'I have a bad feeling about this,' Aisling said.

'Hello there, goats. Here's a treat for yer,' Moira sang out, scattering the food scraps on the ground in front of the hairy trio before turning toward the spectators. 'The brown one's terrible smelly.'

'He'll be a billy goat, alright,' Donal said as though he knew all about goats.

'Moira, smile.' Maureen bossed the camera at the ready.

Moira, never able to resist her turn in front of a camera, struck a sultry feeding the goat's pose.

Donal, Tom, Quinn, Shay, Roisin, Aisling and even the babby Kiera's eyes widened as Noah put their thoughts into words. 'Why's Mr Billy Goat Gruff rearing up at Aunty Moira like that?'

Aisling and Roisin were the first to act, scrambling to their feet and tossing the remains of the picnic into the plastic bags.

'Fold the rug up, one of youse,' Aisling said, her voice unnaturally high.

Down by the river, Maureen's voice rang out clear as a bell, 'Put that thing away, you dirty goat. Don't be waving it at my daughter. Put it away, do you hear me!'

Moira looked like she was doing the Charleston as she waved her hands and kicked her legs about the place trying to ward the frisky Billy goat off.

'Take a step toward me now, Moira. That's it. Easy does it. Now run!'

The two women galloped back to the group nearly tripping over their own feet as they looked over their shoulders to see if the goat was giving chase. To their immense relief he'd decided to try his luck with the white nanny goat instead.

Roisin covered her son's eyes and marched him back to the lane along with the rest of the group.

It was Aisling who began to snigger first once they'd put distance between themselves and the hole in the hedge. The rest of them, with the exception of Maureen and Moira, soon joined in. Even Kiera was clapping her hands delightedly. Noah, however, was confused.

'Mummy, was the Billy Gruff goat trying to sit on the white goat like Mr Nibbles did with Steve?' he asked, setting them all off again.

Roisin decided to seize the moment as they neared the stone bridge and she slowed her pace. 'Shay, we need to talk.'

Shay eyed her curiously. 'That sounds ominous.'

She shook her head. 'It's not. I promise.' Maureen was looking back at them and Roisin waved her on. 'We'll catch you up!' Then, she turned her back on her mammy and the rest of the family to grip the stone wall because her stomach was suddenly amass with butterflies. *Breathe in slowly through your nose, breathe out slowly through your mouth*, she repeated, her nostrils flaring gently as she inhaled. Not once had she factored nerves into the equation when she'd held her imaginary conversations with Shay.

'Rosi, are you okay?'

Roisin exhaled, her lips puckered slightly as though sucking on a straw. She nodded and forced herself to turn and look up at Shay.

His fingers were featherlike as they brushed her cheek. 'You sure?'

'I'm sure.'

'So, come on. This is me, Rosi. What is it?'

Roisin swallowed and blah! Out it came in a jumble of I'm moving to Ireland and I want you to move in with me and Noah, oh and I'd like us to try for a baby too. By the time she'd finished she was as surprised as Shay by the words that had tumbled forth and was giddy with the relief of having got it off her chest. The air around them suddenly smelled sharper, the scent of the grass from the fields sweet and the babbling of the brook like chatter. A silly grin spread across her face as she waited for his reply.

Shay took a little step back from her and held up a hand. 'Whoa slow down there, Rosi.'

'Sorry.' Roisin searched his face but he was giving nothing away.

'Okay, so let me get this straight. You want to move back to Dublin?'

Roisin nodded. 'I do. There's nothing keeping me and Noah in London now Colin's moving to Dubai. I think it will be good for him, for me to be closer to family.' Her smile was almost shy. 'And you. I love you, Shay, and I'm sick of always saying goodbye.'

'And you want us to get a place together?'

'Howth would be lovely. Something small and cosy within walking distance to school for Noah.'

'You've obviously been thinking about this.'

'I have.' Why couldn't she read him? The fluttering nerves were giving way to churning uncertainty. Maybe Shay liked things the way they were. Maybe he liked being committed without being fully committed. He might not feel the need to change a thing between them.

'And you want to try for a baby?'

Oh God, she'd gone too far, she thought, not meeting his gaze as she dipped her head in acknowledgement. It was too late now though, she'd said what she'd said. She couldn't very well take it all back. Why did she have to go so far? Why couldn't she have suggested they move in with one another and see how things went? That would have been more like the easy osi Rosi he knew. They were pointless questions.

He ran his fingers through his hair, his stare intent. 'But you're not proposing to me?'

'What do you mean?'

'You're not proposing in a let's get married way? I'm just trying to get things straight in my mind.'

Roisin shook her head furiously, 'Ah, Jaysus, no! Not at all.' She paused and thought about it. 'Well, I am in a way, I suppose. I mean, I'm proposing things to you.'

There was light dancing in Shay's eyes, and he was biting his bottom lip in an effort not to laugh.

'Shay, I'm after wearing my heart on my sleeve here. It's not funny.'

'Sorry.' He turned Roisin gently toward him, taking both her hands in his. 'I love you, Roisin.'

She held her breath because was it a 'but' or a 'yes' coming?

'And it's a yes to your proposal.'

'But it wasn't a proposal as such.'

Shay laughed and picked her up, swinging her about. 'It's a yes to all of it.'

'Yes? To moving in with myself and Noah and trying for a baby?'

'Yes.'

'Yes!' Roisin flung her head back, feeling the sunshine on her face before slapping his shoulders for him to put her down because it was only right a deal like this was sealed with a kiss.

Chapter Thirty-one

The consensus about the bar area, which had been cleared of tables to allow for dancing, was that the meal had gone over very well, all things considered. Isaac's Hotel had served up a two-course meal of a roast beef main and Irish apple cake and cream for afters. But it was a shame Paudie had been greedy and asked for a second serving of the roasty potatoes, a request that had been declined by yer man who lurked behind the curtains. And, of course, it would have been nice too if Geordie's speech before they tucked into their dinner thanking Noreen for bringing them all together like so hadn't droned on so long that the gravy was beginning to get a skin on it. But all and all, they couldn't complain.

The chatter hummed, and glasses clinked as Donal tapped the microphone several times before breathing into it, 'Testing, testing, one, two, three.'

Maureen, standing by her man, rattled her tambourine and did arm circles warming up while Shay fiddled with his, er, fiddle.

Roisin was standing alongside Suzie, hiding behind Cliona and Orla because Uncle Bartley had taken a shine to Suzie. It wasn't surprising, given how gorgeous she looked in her silky cerise dress. Roisin stood on tiptoes and waved over the top of Cliona's head at Shay. He caught and held her gaze, a secret smile shared between them. They'd decided to hold on to their news until after Colin had spoken to Noah once they returned to London. It wasn't going to be easy keeping things secret because Mammy was a veritable rabbit when it came to digging where secrets were concerned, but they owed it to Noah.

She mused over how funny life could be, raising her glass and sipping on the vinegary liquid. If anyone had told her when her marriage imploded, she'd be sitting in a hotel bar in the village of Claredoncally with all her extended family and the man she'd always dreamed of, so full of happiness two years later... Well, she never would have believed it.

'A one, a two, a one, two, three, four.' Donal was tapping his foot, and Shay began fiddling with the familiar opening bars of the song requested by Noreen. The crowd started yee-haaing and hawing like they were all from Nashville, Tennessee, instead of Ireland.

Donal looked deep into Maureen's eyes and Maureen into his as she shook her tambourine, and they began their serenade. Glen peeled off the wall he was leaning against and whispered something to Suzie, who nodded, and Roisin watched as he held out his hand for Dara.

Dara's tremulous joy at being led onto the dance floor area by her son saw tears well in Roisin's eyes. Suzie's, too, were glistening.

Noah's sudden appearance was a distraction as he pulled at the skirt of her dress. 'Come on, Mummy.' She followed him out into the huddle, and holding both his hands in hers, they swayed to the music.

Uncle Bartley, forever fickle in his affections, was cutting his moves in front of Freya, who was feigning interest in the floor. Aisling dragged Moira and Suzie out onto the floor and rescued her.

Roisin smiled as Noah stood on her toes, and they proceeded to do a sort of waltz.

Her heart was fit to burst. She was going home.

THE END

There are more O'Mara family shenanigans coming soon in...

The O'Maras go Greek – Book 14, The Guesthouse on the Green series

Out 1 July 2023

Welcome to the guesthouse on the Green, where Mammy and her girls will make you feel part of the family. Settle in and enjoy your stay at O'Mara's, where stories abound, romance lurks and laughter sounds.

If you've ever fancied visiting Santorini in the Greek Islands, now is your chance because Patrick O'Mara is about to wed Cindy. She might be the woman of Patrick's dreams, but the wedding destination is not the stuff of Mammy O'Mara's dreams. What's wrong with a church wedding in Ireland? She can't be doing with all this barefoot on the beach nonsense. Still and all, it's an excuse for a family holiday, and she is all about family. You're family too, so what are you waiting for? Pack your bags. We've got a wedding to go to!

Thanks so much for reading An O'Mara's Reunion. If you enjoyed this latest instalment in the O'Mara family's lives please recommend the books to other readers and leave a review or starred rating on Amazon or Goodreads. I'd so appreciate it!

About Author

Michelle Vernal lives in Christchurch, New Zealand with her husband, two teenage sons and attention seeking tabby cats, Humphrey and Savannah. Before she started writing novels, she had a variety of jobs:

Pharmacy shop assistant, girl who sold dried up chips and sausages at a hot food stand in a British pub, girl who sold nuts (for 2 hours) on a British market stall, receptionist, P.A...Her favourite job though is the one she has now – writing stories she hopes leave her readers with a satisfied smile on their face.

If you'd like to know when Michelle's next book is coming out you can visit www.michellevernalbooks.com or say hello on her Facebook page at www.facebook.com/michellevernalnovelist

Books by Michelle Vernal

♥

The Cooking School on the Bay
Second-hand Jane
Staying at Eleni's
The Traveller's Daughter
Sweet Home Summer
When We Say Goodbye
And...

Series fiction

<u>The Guesthouse on the Green Series</u>

Book 1 - O'Mara's
Book 2 – Moira-Lisa Smile
Book 3 – What goes on Tour
Book 4 – Rosi's Regrets
Book 5 – Christmas at O'Mara's
Book 6 – A Wedding at O'Mara's
Book 7 – Maureen's Song

Book 8 – The O'Maras in LaLa Land

Book 9 – Due in March

Book 10 – A Baby at O'Mara's

Book 11 – The Housewarming

Book 12 – Rainbows over O'Mara's

Book 13 – An O'Mara's Reunion

Book 14 – The O'Maras go Greek - Out July 2023

Liverpool Brides Series

The Autumn Posy

The Winter Posy

The Spring Posy

The Summer Posy

Isabel's Story

The Promise

The Letter

Christmas in the Little Irish Village

Book 2 coming in May 2023